Suddenly, Jessie heard a commotion beyond the walls of Billy's room. It sounded like cursing and yelling and flesh striking flesh. Alarmed, drawing her weapon, Jessie stood.

"What is it?" Billy cried.

Jessie opened the door just a crack. She froze.

The saloon was filled with thirty or forty men, many of them dressed in the uniform of the Confederacy. One of them, a tall, broad man in a black leather coat that reached to his knees, announced, "Everyone relax and no one gets hurt. General Misery has arrived in Hell to save the day . . . Okay, people, bottom line here, I'm in charge now. Anyone have a problem with that?"

Jessie closed the door, her heart pounding with fear. She looked at Billy and asked, "Is there another way out of here?"

Billy jerked a nod. "Yes. What's wrong? Who are these men?"

"Demons."

DON'T MISS THESE
ALL-ACTION WESTERN SERIES
FROM THE BERKLEY PUBLISHING GROUP

THE GUNSMITH by J. R. Roberts

Clint Adams was a legend among lawmen, outlaws, and ladies. They called him . . . the Gunsmith.

LONGARM by Tabor Evans

The popular long-running series about U.S. Deputy Marshal Long—his life, his loves, his fight for justice.

LONE STAR by Wesley Ellis

The blazing adventures of Jessica Starbuck and the martial arts master, Ki. Over eight million copies in print.

SLOCUM by Jake Logan

Today's longest-running action Western. John Slocum rides a deadly trail of hot blood and cold steel.

→◆→ **WESLEY ELLIS** ◆←

LONE STAR

AND A SALOON CALLED HELL

JOVE BOOKS, NEW YORK

LONE STAR AND A SALOON CALLED HELL

A Jove Book / published by arrangement with
the author

PRINTING HISTORY
Jove edition / July 1994

ISBN: 0-515-11408-1

A JOVE BOOK®
Jove Books are published by The Berkley Publishing Group,
200 Madison Avenue, New York, New York 10016.
JOVE and the "J" design are trademarks belonging
to Jove Publications, Inc.

PRINTED IN THE UNITED STATES OF AMERICA

10 9 8 7 6 5 4 3 2 1

LONE STAR

AND A SALOON
CALLED HELL

★

Chapter 1

She had a growing sense of foreboding, of impending death hanging in the cold air, and her mind wanted to warn her that there were ghosts in the thick mist, unseen demons lurking, hiding, waiting to devour her.

No, it *was* all in her mind, the festering torment of the past gripping her with terrible and haunting memories, feeding her fear of nothing and everything. There was nothing out there but the mountains and the cold and her dread that nothing would ever be right and good again.

All Jessica Starbuck could say right then was that she and her longtime bodyguard and companion, Ki, were deep in Wyoming Territory. They had ridden for weeks, slogging through the snow and the mud, braving the cold, rationing their food and their water, heading north, deeper and deeper into the cold and the mountains and the

1

unforgiving freezing shroud of winter that clung to the air like the devil's breath. For days they had seen no one and nothing, not even a moose or a bear or a deer. It was eerie.

The world was silent. Even though the sun's rays pierced through the shroud of fog blanketing the valley of the Grand Tetons, the world looked and felt dead to Jessie.

Even though she was wrapped in a thick black bearskin coat, black leather pants, black leather boots, and a white wool shirt, she shivered. She wondered if she shivered from the cold, or from the creepy atmosphere around her.

And her heart felt heavy as stone, but soft still for whenever the new life of the spring of love flowered again.

Lately, though, she wondered if there was anything good left in life. All that now remained was her .44 Colt, Winchester rifle, and hunting knife. And there was a new addition to her weaponry. It was a bullwhip, curled around the saddle horn, sleek and black, a long leather snake that could sting an enemy with agonizing poison. She shrugged the coat higher up on her shoulders, pulled the brim of her black Stetson farther down on her forehead.

Beside Jessie, his own black gelding trudging through the thick snow, Ki, dressed in a long sheepskin coat, black wool pants, leather vest, and black Stetson, looked at Jessie, concern in his eyes. Letting out a long breath, Ki kept his leather-gloved hand wrapped around the butt of his .44 Remington, the stock of a Winchester rifle jutting up from a scabbard on the other side. Sheathed inside his black leather sash was his samurai sword, his *katana*, honed to razor sharpness. Inside his vest were dozens of *shurikens*, razor-edged, star-shaped steel disks that were deadly in Ki's hands.

"Kindly stop that," Jessie said.

"Kindly stop what?"

"The sighing. The looks. Your worrying about me."

Ki shook his head. Where was the old Jessie, who was so full of life, looking forward to each and every day as something to be cherished, to all life as precious and dear? When was the last time he had even seen her smile?

"And stop shaking your head. I'm all right."

Ki let it ride. "We need food, Jess. All we know is that we're heading north for this town, a new hell on our horizon, and everything's gone. Aren't you hungry?"

"Not really."

Ki scowled.

They plodded through the snow for another endless few hours of silence. Then they saw a cabin, slowly emerging through the mist, at the edge of a stand of trees. Black smoke curled from the stone chimney.

There was someone standing in front of the cabin. Judging by the long white hair, the shape of the body in a fur coat and black leather dress, Jessie suspected they rode up on the back side of a woman. Without moving the head, the figure turned, and Jessie saw the large firm breasts,

3

nipples distended against the sheer fabric of a black blouse. Strange how the woman did not turn their way, she thought, only swivel her whole body without her head moving. She just stood there, in front of a fire that burned beneath a large black pot.

Jessie and Ki stopped several yards behind the woman. "Hello?" she said.

No answer. Jessie looked at Ki. Something felt wrong.

The mist suddenly swirled, but there was no wind. Jessie shivered.

"Hello?"

The woman turned, and Jessie had to fight down her gasp of surprise.

"Do not be afraid," the woman said in a gentle voice.

Jessie stared at the woman's face. There was nothing but whiteness where her eyes should have been. The woman's face betrayed no age. Her hair was as white as snow, the skin of her face so white and pure, she appeared like an angel. No, Jessie thought, she had the face of a child.

"Yes, I am blind," she said. "But I see more now than when I had eyes. Indeed, I can see more than most of us ever do with sight."

Jessie stared at this woman, mesmerized, afraid. She had never seen a face with an expression of so much serenity and peace.

"I—we didn't mean to startle you," Jessie told her.

She smiled. "Is it you who startle me? Really."

Jessie balked, ashamed of herself for a moment. "My name is Jessie."

"I am Ki."

The strange woman nodded. "I am Cassandra. Some think I am a witch, some say I am a prophetess. I live alone here. My husband died many years ago. I feel you are curious about my eyes. I do not take offense that you stare."

"I'm sorry—"

"Do not be. Blindness has given me sight into many things that before I could not see. I have been blind for so long—I almost have forgotten—I remember now, I tell you to satisfy your curiosity, to ease your fear. You see, there was an explosion of kerosene in the home where I lived with my husband. The fire erupted, just several feet from my face. I was not burned. I was only blinded by the fire. They tell me my eyes are as white as snow. It can be frightening, at first. I feel the reaction of all who see me, but men have also told me that I am more beautiful than any woman they have ever seen. I am alone and I need to know life. I need to hear a human voice. I long for a kind word. When you are alone so much as I, your world shrinks every day, and madness is never far. So, tell me, am I as they say?"

Jessie didn't know how to answer that, but Ki told the woman, "Yes. You are perhaps the most beautiful woman I have ever seen. I mean that."

A warm smile crossed the woman's ageless face. "I believe you. And thank you, kind sir. However, be that as it may, words that speak from the human heart, especially words that are kind and gentle and sincere, are as fleeting as a breath of air. I am what I am, an old blind woman who has either been blessed or cursed with the gift of the sight of the unknown. You see, after the accident, people feared what happened to me. It could not be explained how I was not burned." She shrugged. "My husband and I were chased and hunted for some time by—well, not very long ago they were called witch hunters. The fear and the pain were too much for him to bear. He drank himself to death. He choked on his own vomit." She paused. "As you will, too, Jessie, if you do not let go of your suffering."

Jessie felt fear ripple through her. "How—"

"Ssshhh. You are hungry. Get down off your horses, please. Come close. Let me feel what is in your souls."

They dismounted, Jessie feeling drawn to this woman's power.

Cassandra gently put her hands on the faces of Jessie and Ki. Sorrow hardened the blind woman's face.

"It is as I sensed. You both are in great pain.

"Yes, yes," Cassandra breathed. "There is great power in both of you. You have good hearts, kind hearts, but there is the rage of violence there. You are—how shall I say—people of destiny. You look for someone—a man? No, a boy—someone you knew."

Jessie pulled away. How did the woman know this?

"You are frightened, Jessie?"

"How—?"

6

"Tell me about the one you look for."

Jessie tried to get her mouth to work. Finally, she said, "I—you know? Have—has anyone come by here recently?"

"Not the one you seek. The one you seek, he is in trouble. I sense he is not an old lover, but someone you care deeply for."

Jessie suddenly felt compelled to tell this woman the truth of their passing this way. "Yes. A young man. His name is Billy Johnson. I—I took him into my home, years ago. He was raised by his mother. The father left them when he was born. Billy's father was an outlaw, a bad man, and he was killed in a saloon. The mother was abusive to the boy. She beat him terribly. Finally—well, she—killed herself. With a knife, she cut her own throat. The boy, he found his own mother—like that. You can imagine his suffering. I took it upon myself to raise Billy. He was bright and sensitive, but very troubled. I treated him like a mother should a son."

"And this boy, he—he wrote poetry, I believe."

"Y-yes, he did."

"To ease his hurt soul, to relieve his suffering, to not feel so alone and unwanted in the world. I understand."

"Yes."

"Go on."

"He—when Billy was older and becoming more uncontrollable, he would drink, more and more, he—stole money from me to drink and to whore and to gamble. It happened more than once. One time, even four or five times, I could forgive. I saw

7

I couldn't help him. I told him he had to leave my home. It broke my heart. I still feel some degree of guilt over that. Now—now, I hear, he is being hunted for murder. I heard he had fled to this territory."

"You cannot save the world, Jessie, much less one boy, much less yourself. You have tasted the powers of hell in your suffering. You should know this."

Jessie became angry. "That doesn't mean I'll ever quit trying to help someone I care for."

"Of course not. Tell me more. But inside."

Cassandra turned, and it was then that Jessie noticed she wore no shoes. How could she not even shiver or feel the freezing cold on her bare feet? Jessie felt afraid to go on, but even more afraid not to know more about the blind woman. Cassandra knew something, she sensed, something very important, and Jessie had to know what the blind woman saw in her dark world of utter isolation and loneliness, in the world of the unseen.

They followed the blind woman into her cabin. The place was immaculate, lit brightly by dozens of candles. Furs of bears and mountain lions lined the floor and the walls. Fire crackled from a cast-iron stove in the far corner. The walls were lined with vials and pouches, and there were leather-bound books with strange symbols on the bindings. There were several pipes, or bowls with stems, and these were made of glass. There was a thick brown caking of residue on the inside of these glass pipes.

Whatever she had been smoking, some smell lingered in the air. The place smelled faintly of herbs.

"Yes," she said, ladling something from a black pot, pouring the broth into three bowls. With deft fingers, she ground dozens of small leaves into pulp, sprinkling them in the bowls. "I know the powder, I know the light and the darkness of the powder, and other things from it I have created. Just as you have, Jessie. However, I will not put temptation before you. That is not the reason you're here. Eat this. It will give you strength and energy. I will fix you some to take with you."

Jessie saw a strange look in Ki's eyes. Ki appeared hypnotized by this blind woman, falling under her strange spell. Lately, perhaps because of her mood swings, Ki was silent and distant in Jessie's presence, but something was happening to Ki and Jessie sensed it had nothing to do with her.

"Sit and eat."

They did. The broth was strong, and it tasted of the same herbs Jessie whiffed in the air. It tasted sweet but bitter.

"What is this stuff?" Ki asked.

Cassandra smiled. "I believe Jessie already has some idea."

"The Medicine Man?"

"Yes. Once in a great while, he passes this way."

As she ate the broth, Jessie felt strength and energy surge through her body, her hunger vanishing.

"The boy you seek—" Cassandra said. "There is a town, a place north of here, perhaps a day's ride in good weather. It is called Apocalypse. For a long time God-fearing people lived there. They were slain by evil men not very long ago. There is no longer any law of man or God there. Before bad men took the town, it was called something else, I do not know now. They changed the name to mock the dead. Now, there is much evil there, and even good men are afraid to venture in. Perhaps you will find the boy there. If he is hiding there, then it may well be all is lost for him. Evil men are like a contagious disease; they contaminate everything they come into contact with. Good that is not strong will be infected by them. If this boy is as troubled as you say, I fear for him. And for you. Your heart, I fear, cannot bear up to much more suffering."

Jessie said nothing. If what this woman said was true, and she had no reason to doubt her word, they would ride for Apocalypse.

They ate in silence. Finally, Jessie thanked the blind woman and told her they had to go. The woman nodded, said she understood, wished them luck, and handed Jessie a small pot of the strange broth that gave energy and strength and killed hunger. Then she made a strange request. She asked Jessie to step outside, leave her alone with Ki for a minute.

Jessie waited outside. What did Cassandra want with Ki?

Jessie mounted her horse. Finally, Ki walked outside. Jessie looked at him, wanting to know what had happened, but not wanting to appear too curious. The relationship between the two of them was strained at best these days.

"Ki? Are you all right?"

The look in Ki's eyes disturbed Jessie. He looked haunted, but wild with desire.

"I'm fine."

"What did she want?"

"She—she asked me—to come back at some point later. She said she—well, she wants to know my power. That she can be the healing of my soul."

Jessie didn't know what to say.

Ki mounted. "You know—she kissed me—just one time. But I felt something like I have never felt in my life. It was as if electricity passed through my body when she kissed me. I felt some charge—some rush of pure power."

Jessie knew Ki would come back here. Suddenly, she was afraid for him. Pure power for anything human, whether in passion, in law, or in the gun or gold, she had discovered, is the final fatal trap of the proud.

★

Chapter 2

Another long night of cold and silence passed, as Jessie and Ki slept, huddled close to a fire. When dawn came and the sun rose, they continued to ride north through the same soundless white mist. As the sun shone brighter, the mist and the snow seemed to blend into one blinding, impenetrable curtain. Jessie squinted into the silent whiteness around them.

Later she found herself lapsing into the same brooding hardness as the day before, and the day before that. Troubled thoughts preyed on her mind, sorrow burned in her heart.

She told Ki, "It all comes and it all goes, doesn't it, Ki. It all goes on, it has to."

"Jessie, oh, God, Jessie, like Cassandra said, you must somehow let go of your heartache, or it will kill you."

"I hope—in time."

Suddenly, there was the soft whicker of a horse. Startled, Jessie turned in the saddle. To the west, a figure on horseback appeared, white on white in the mist. Jessie peered, reined in her mount.

The man was big in the saddle, and he appeared like a ghostly apparition at first, sliding through the mist, dressed in a long heavy white coat, white Stetson, black Levi's, and black boots. He rode the biggest, most beautiful white gelding Jessie had ever seen. As he neared, Jessie stared at his face. He was not a handsome man; in fact, he was damn near ugly, Jessie thought, with a big-boned face, thick gray stubble, white hair flowing to his shoulders, gray eyes that were hard and cold, and several livid knife scars around his mouth and the corner of his left eye. He had the look of a cold-blooded killer. His hand was draped over the butt of a .44 Colt. He just sat there in the saddle, staring back at Jessie and Ki. He reached into his saddlebag, pulled out a thick stack of wanted posters. He leafed through the papers, then grunted.

He smiled coldly. "No money, no honey."

He rode on, angling to the north.

Jessie watched him vanish into the mist. She shivered. Those cold gray eyes lingered in her mind, a vision of death.

Silently, waiting for the stranger in white to put some distance ahead of them, Jessie and Ki rode in his wake.

Perhaps two hours later, another building in the white wilderness appeared out of the mist. It was a small cabin with a hitching post. Beside three tired-looking black geldings, the man in white slid off his saddle, tied his white horse to the railing, and moved inside the cabin, his saddlebag filled with bounty papers draped over his shoulder.

Jessie saw the sign that read TRADING POST. They needed to resupply, so they dismounted, and also went inside.

They stood by the door, scanning the cramped room. A fire burned from a cast-iron stove, the shadows of flame dancing over the heavily bearded, hard-eyed faces of three men gathered around a table in the far corner. The stranger in white walked to the counter where an old, stoop-shouldered, toothless man watched with fear in his eyes. The stranger in the white coat was over six feet tall and weighed over two hundred solid pounds. His presence seemed to fill the room. The three men watched him, and Jessie read the fear in their eyes as well.

"Help you, sir?" the old man said.

The air was thick with tension, the smells of leather, fire, and cigar smoke a cloying stink that hung like a cloud in the room.

Silence. Nothing but the crackling of the fire.

"No," the stranger in white said.

A grunt from one of the three men.

Slowly, side by side, Jessie and Ki moved to the counter. She sensed the burning, lustful stares of the men behind her. The stranger showed the trio a cold smile.

"They call me Barabbas."

The one in the middle of the threesome nodded, stroked his red beard. "We know who you are. And we know what you are. You've been following us. We're here. You're here. Let's do it."

One of them was sucking on a thick wad of tobacco. He squished out a long stream that spattered on the floor, just inches from the boots of Barabbas. The big man looked down at his boots, his expression mean.

Jessie just watched, her heart pounding in her ears, her hand close to her Colt revolver.

"I just bought these boots from a Shoshone as old as God," Barabbas told the trio. "They cost me three bottles of whiskey and a pouch of tobacco. Now, kindly listen to my tale of the boots, for I suffered much aggravation to acquire them. You see, the old Shoshone, he owns a white whore, and she insisted on money for his time and his talent. She tells him, 'No money, no honey.' She must've said that ten, maybe twelve times while I was there. I mean, the whole time I'm there, waiting while he makes my boots, this whore, she's whining and pissing and moaning and scowling and sulking. I know the deal, I feel sorry for him. So, I offered him cash because they were the last of my whiskey and my smokes at the time. I could see he was tired of the white whore, a tiresome and whining and spoiled creature, she was. He slapped her and she shut up, barking that he would rather have the whiskey and the tobacco instead of her tired white ass. I can understand that; a man's got to get his priorities right sometimes. Hell, he even offers me her mouth and for free, but I wasn't interested. Mind you, this is nothing but a white whore, I know this. Now, I could add that no self-respecting white man would have a damn thing to do with her anyway, but that's a little mean-spirited on my part, and I'm really just a gentle live-and-let-live soul. Anyway, he goes on to shame his whore more still, as he should, telling her she is like all white women he has known, that her heart is full of mischief and deception and vile desires, that the beauty of the white woman goes no deeper than her skin. I shrug. I know there are exceptions to everything, that one cannot make these sweeping condemnations without casting some judgment on themselves. So, point is, after all that wheeling and dealing and spieling, I'm proud of these boots—plus I passed up a free piece of ass, thus saving my self-respect and honor and dignity."

After the tale of the boots and the story of the salvaging of his pride, the spitter spat again, this time splattering the prized footwear. The spitter's comrades chuckled.

Barabbas laughed a strange laugh. He reached into his saddlebag.

The trio tensed, their hands falling beneath the table.

"Easy, boys. Are you that scared of me? I am only one. You are three."

"We ain't scared of jackshit," the man with the red beard said.

"Good. So, relax. I just want to show you something."

Barabbas walked to their table. He dropped three wanted posters on the table between their bottles and their cards.

"Willie Peebles, how do you do?" Barabbas said to the man with the red beard. "Rapist, killer, and thief. What we got here is generally just more shit taking up space in an ever-shrinking world. Got to tell you, Willie, not a bad likeness, but you're even uglier in person."

"You go to hell," Willie Peebles growled, standing up, unzipping himself, and spraying the posters with a stream of yellow that seemed to go on for minutes.

"Now, why would a man piss on his own face?" Barabbas asked no one in particular. Then, just as Willie was about to tuck himself away, a knife blurred through the air, a vicious swish of metal.

Jessie was rooted with fear, a cry of terror ripping from Willie's mouth, and the old storekeeper gasped, "Jesus God!"

Time froze.

His eyes bulging, trembling, Willie looked down, then sighed, finding himself still all in place.

Barabbas smiled into Willie's eyes. "This could be a first. Never seen a man die with his dick in his hands. Damn, but you do look relieved and amazed. Now I know what you're thinking, Willie. You're thinking, 'How'd he do that so quick, how did he slip that in there when there is so little room to work with?' Pretty astute observation, wouldn't you say, Willie? Like that word? Astute? Of course, you don't, you dumb bastard, you don't even know what it means. Don't anybody move!" he growled at Willie's buddies. "Here's what I want, and I might spare your lives. A boy, about twenty. Blond and short and skinny. Heard him

18

described as goofy-looking, sad face and sad eyes, not the best lookin' guy around, but hey, I ain't real pretty myself. Kid drinks a lot, smokes. Hear he's a poet, too. Anybody like that read some poetry to you lately? Boys?"

Jessie listened with sudden alarm.

"He goes by the name of Jamie, or Tommy sometimes," Barabbas continued. "He is on the run. He is wanted for murder. I understand he was with you only a few short weeks ago. I understand he was headed this way. So, tell me, where is he? Willie? I'm waiting."

"He—yeah—he was with us."

"And?"

"He—stole some money from us. We was asleep. The little shit! We find him, he's dead."

"Oh?"

Barabbas pulled the blade away, fast. Willie shrieked. When he found himself still whole, he collapsed in his chair.

"I don't want you three, anyway," Barabbas said. Turning his back on them, he strode toward the counter. "You aren't even worth a week's whiskey binge to me."

"You bastard!" Willie screamed, jumping to his feet, his comrades drawing iron and leaping up beside him.

They died, fast, hard, and bloody. Wheeling, Barabbas's gun flamed three times. Thunder rolled, and bullets tore into their chests, flinging them behind a cloud of shredded cloth and flying blood, hammering them into the wall. They crumpled, slid down the wall, eyes wide in death.

19

Stunned by his speed, Jessie stared at the bounty hunter. He touched the brim of his hat.

"Ma'am, my apologies," he told Jessie. "I don't like working my trade in front of ladies." He looked at the old man. "Whiskey, whatever meat you got, plenty of tobacco, and cheroots. Let's do the works. Whenever I start running low on whiskey and smokes, well, I can be a little mean."

Shaking, the old man got the bounty hunter what he wanted. "It's on the house, sir."

Barabbas was toeing the dead, then wiped his boots off on Willie, the spitter. He moved back to the counter.

"Uh-uh. I pay my own way. No," he said, looking over his shoulder at the twitching dead. "On second thought, you can trade them in. We're even. Ma'am, sir," he nodded to Jessie and Ki. "I'll see you in Hell, maybe."

Without another word, the bounty hunter named Barabbas walked out into the silent white mist. A sudden gust of howling wind blew past the bounty hunter, then the door shut with a bang.

Jessie looked at Ki, knew that he knew what she was thinking. She told the old man what they needed, then they left to follow the bounty hunter.

"Hey! Hey, you!"

Ki followed Jessie, her angry call echoing into the white mist. Barabbas reined his mount in to face her. Ki was afraid of what Jessie might do. For some time now there was something deadly and reckless just beneath the surface of the beauty of this woman. It was as if she purposely sought confrontation, craved to throw her life in danger.

Barabbas fired up a cheroot, gruffed, "Help you, lady?"

Jessie stopped hard, the hooves of her horse throwing a cloud of snow over the bounty hunter. Barabbas calmly brushed himself off.

"Give it up," Jessie said.

"Give what up, lady?"

"The kid. Forget him."

Barabbas puffed his cheroot around his cold smile. "What's the kid to you, lady? What do you care?"

"I don't need to tell you a thing, mister. Except this. You harm that boy, I will kill you. You will die in pain—great pain."

Barabbas's gaze narrowed. He nodded. "I believe you."

Hard silence.

Ki watched, sitting tense and ready in the saddle next to Jessie.

"You people got names? Like to know who I'm dealing with here."

Jessie didn't answer that. "Your name really Barabbas?"

"Just like the rabble-rouser and malcontent ol' Pontius handed over to the mob."

"What I said," Jessie growled.

"What you said don't mean a damn thing to me. You listen, lady, you, too, pal. For one thing, I don't want the kid. Not the way you think I do. There's bigger fish out there, the kid's not even a tadpole. My thinking is, he did something stupid, but he's harmless. Thing is, he's young and probably doesn't know nearly as much as he thinks he does. The deal is, and this is purely guesswork, he's hiding somewhere, probably in this shithole north of here called Apocalypse. Maybe he's being protected. Who knows! Maybe some hard-luck case will take him down and turn him in for a bottle of whiskey or a night with a whore. As time passes, the bounty on him goes up. Time for the booty to get nice and fat. Plenty of time for the wrong guy to have his blade real sharp and ready."

"Make your point," Ki said.

"My point is, bad men will come after him. Now, I can see the kid means something to you, what it is, I don't know, don't really care. Bottom line, I can keep the kid alive."

"Why?" Jessie sneered. "So you can use him to lure in the bigger fish?"

Barabbas just smiled and puffed. "If you were a man, I'd say you have balls." He seemed to search his mind. "You know, if I didn't know better, I'd guess you two are the Lone Star Legend. Jessie Starbuck and her sidekick, Ki."

Ki tensed. "What the lady said. Any different, and I'll show you sidekick."

"I believe you would, Ki." A hard pause. "Okay, now that the introductions are over, now what?"

"We ride," Jessie said.

"Oh, just like that, I let you two tag along?"

Jessie and Ki said nothing.

Barabbas pitched his cheroot away, shrugged,

said, "What the hell. Why not? Just don't crowd me."

Another stretched second of silence, then Barabbas wheeled his mount around. Jessie and Ki fell in beside the bounty hunter.

★

Chapter 3

The white buildings of the town appeared suddenly, almost out of nowhere, slowly rising out of the mist. They stopped at the edge of a rise, staring down into the valley of Apocalypse. Jessie looked at the small wooden sign that announced the town's name in red letters. Whether the word had been scrawled in paint or blood, Jessie didn't know, but she suspected it was probably the latter. For beside the sign was a dead horse and the body of a man, his eyes wide in death. Icicles had long since formed on his beard and eyebrows, and a trail of crimson led from the black gaping maw across his throat to the sign.

"Nice place for a little holiday, huh," Barabbas grunted.

Silence hung over the town. Except for the black skeleton of a church at the north end of town, hulking in the middle of a snow-covered street that bisected two rows of structures, every building was stark white, and the town could appear invisible in the mist and the snow at first glance. Rising above the mist was a cross atop the charred shell of a steeple, the cross somehow having survived the torch job to the sacred haven of the faithful.

Struck by the words and tone of Barabbas, for a moment Jessie stared at the bounty hunter. This man was brutal and cold, and money was perhaps his only god. The way he had talked about the Shoshone and his white whore—not so much what he had said, but how he'd told the tale of the boots—led Jessie to believe that this man had no respect for women, much less life. She found herself revolted by Barabbas, but in some strange, perverse way, she was also intrigued. This man was full of demons, full of fatal pride, with not a shred of kindness or decency that she could detect. He seemed to fit in well with the world as Jessie saw it. Lately, she felt like that, too.

Silently, they rode into Apocalypse. The town appeared deserted, but as they slid through the mist, Jessie saw several dozen horses hitched to a long railing in front of a saloon.

"Welcome to Hell," the bounty hunter said, as they pulled up in front of the saloon.

Across the large plate-glass window, in bold red letters, was painted HELL. Beneath the word, scrawled in white letters, was: 'Abandon hope all ye who enter here.'

The bounty hunter read that part, grunted, said, "Obviously someone with either a morbid sense of humor, or someone with a profound sense of the religious, or maybe the two are one and the same thing. Very interesting. Well. Shall we?"

Suddenly, the door to Hell burst open. A man tumbled across the boardwalk. He tried to stand, but his pants were down around his ankles, and he toppled, desperately trying to cover his partial nakedness. A stunning redhead strode through the doorway. Except for a pair of black leather boots, she was naked. She was tall, close to six and a half feet tall. The nipples on her large, firm breasts were like thimbles, distended, pointing like small weapons against the freezing air. There was a Winchester rifle canted to her shoulder. With contempt she stared down at the partly naked man, who trembled in terror or awe at the fearsome, mesmerizing sight of this stunning redhead. The guy tried to stand again, but she kicked him square in the face. Jessie flinched as blood sprayed from his nose. Through the plate-glass window of the saloon, Jessie saw bearded faces with laughing eyes.

"I—I'm sorry," the guy whimpered.

"You're sorry, all right," the redhead laughed. "Stand up!"

He stood.

"Leave your pants down!"

He did.

"Here's what I think of you wanting a free ride on Stacey's tab," she said.

With no more thought than she might give to stepping on a cockroach, she shot him in the arm. The guy howled in agony, clutching his mangled limb. Then the redhead cranked out six, then seven, then eight shots, shredding the guy from crotch to sternum, pinning him to the beam, making him dance a jig of death for her. A smile stretched her full red lips as she kept pumping him full of lead, making him twitch, scream, and bounce all over for her delight. Jessie and Ki watched in cold fear and revulsion, as the man slowly turned their way, his face etched in the eternal mask of agonizing death. He seemed to stand before Jessie for a stretched second, staring her in the eye, wisps of gunsmoke curling past his death mask before he crumpled to the street, his ass bared to the now howling mob in the saloon called Hell.

Barabbas whistled, smiled at the redhead. "I think I'm in love."

With contempt, the redhead, canting the rifle across her breasts, glared at Barabbas. "Bar of soap inside you can fall in love with. Help yourself."

She wheeled and vanished inside Hell.

Jessie, Ki, and Barabbas dismounted. Jessie took the bullwhip, hung it around her shoulder. Grinning, Barabbas looked at the whip.

"How about you? Any plans for this evening, ma'am?"

Jessie returned his cold smile. "What did you say earlier? Don't crowd me?"

"Something like that. But can't a man change his mind?"

"Like a woman's prerogative?"

"Right."

"Like the whore said. Help yourself to that bar of soap."

As Jessie moved, something clawed into her leg. Startled, she wrenched herself free of the dead man's grasp, thinking he was convulsing in death throes. As she stared down at him, she saw he wasn't dead. He croaked blood, the most terrible and agonized expression she had ever seen imploring her with, "Help—help me—"

A gun cannoned, and the man's face shattered into bloody pulp.

Jessie wheeled again, found the smoking Colt in the hand of Barabbas. The bounty hunter twirled the gun smoothly, tucked it away in his holster. A vile stench then pierced Jessie's senses. Grimacing, she looked down at the corpse, then knew what had happened.

"Mmmm," Barabbas grunted, making a face. "How do you like that for gratitude? Guy asks for help, I do him a favor, and what does he do? He shits himself. How do you like that?"

Jessie bit down her anger and contempt as she followed the bounty hunter with a mean-eyed stare as he headed for the doors of Hell. Just like that, she made her decision. She wanted to bring that guy to his knees.

They walked into the gloomy bowels of Hell. Inside the doorway, Jessie stood beside Ki while the bounty hunter walked across the room, heading for the long wooden bar in the far corner. There, he snapped his fingers at a tall comely blonde in fur and leather and demanded a bottle of whiskey.

Jessie took it all in, chilled by what she saw and felt. Like good, evil has a presence, a force about it that is powerful and alluring. But when one was faced with the presence of pure evil, it was unforgettable; a look in the eyes of the evil that can burn into the memory and never be forgotten.

Jessie sensed this pervasive evil in Hell.

The kerosene lanterns, hung from beams around the large room, and the fire that crackled and glowed from four cast-iron stoves positioned in all four corners of the saloon, made the patrons' faces shine with that wild, cold, and silent tormented laughter of the wicked. Oil paintings of naked women, or naked women performing various obscene acts, lined the walls.

Jessie could feel the sorrow and the anguish, the desire of the flesh, greed and anger in the air. Men's eyes burned with lust as they stared at her. Men of different ages, dressed in denim and leather and fur, toting sidearms, rifles never far from their fingers. Whiskey bottles were everywhere. Cigarette and cigar smoke wafted across the room like noxious clouds. The blind seer came to Jessie's mind. These people were poison, and, if the bounty hunter's guess was right and Billy Johnson was being hidden by these creatures of darkness, then she feared for him.

Jessie was at once stunned and afraid, revolted and mesmerized. Something warned her she should not stay in this place, that she, too, could easily become corrupted.

The women, some naked with only gold ankle bracelets or necklaces made of diamonds or pearls or jade, others partly clad in fur boots and black leather vests, could bring any man to his knees with lust. Blondes and brunettes, redheads and Spanish women with hair as black as a raven, all of these beauties long-legged and big-breasted, with firm rounded buttocks and full ripe red lips. Sitting or stretched out on divans, smoking and drinking, their eyes were full of laughter and desire. Their nails were painted, and some of their faces were heavily painted, also. The air reeked of perfume and the musky odor of women in heat. Jessie's senses reeled from the sight and the smell.

"Who are you?" asked a blonde. Jessie looked at the woman—girl, really. She appeared to be no more than fifteen or sixteen. Still, she had that look of the wicked in her eyes, her voice a sweet croon.

"Nobody," Jessie said.

Jessie gave the mob one final scathing search. There was no sign of Billy Johnson, but Jessie had expected as much.

Jessie and Ki moved to a table, far away from all of them, but Jessie could still feel them, heavy and burning with desire.

Then Jessie saw him. Had she been somewhere other than a saloon named Hell, she would have laughed out loud.

He filled the doorway behind the bar. He was a brute of a man, and he stood there, stark naked. Fear instantly fell over the room. Fear, she sensed, and a good degree of desire and jealousy.

He was dark-skinned, with long black hair, high cheekbones, dark eyes. He was the biggest Indian Jessie had ever seen, his body looking as if it was carved out of granite.

"They just walked in here, Bull," the comely blonde barmaid said.

Bull had a body as muscular as any Jessie had ever seen. Indeed, every muscle in his body rippled as he strode out from behind the bar. There, he stood, hands on hips, proudly displaying the biggest cock Jessie had ever seen. It hung to his knees. His eyes laughed, as he said, "Like what you see?"

Jessie looked away.

A blonde then practically fell through the doorway behind the bar. She was sweating, disheveled, out of breath.

"Oh, God," she moaned. "I can hardly stand, Bull, God damn you."

"Shut up, whore," Bull growled over his shoulder. "Go get me a bottle, then sit down and wait for me. I'll let you know when I need you again."

She did as she was told. When she handed him a bottle, Bull told Jessie and Ki, "No idea who you people are. But if you come here to get rich, let me show you something that might make you think twice."

"This one, too, Bull," another whore called out, jerking a nod at Barabbas.

"Come here, fella," Bull ordered. "Off your old tired ass."

Barabbas took a deep pull of whiskey. He stood, shrugged, said, "So show me something."

Wisely, Barabbas kept his distance. Bull chuckled at the bounty hunter's obvious anxiety, moved to the far wall. There, he slid back a door. Instantly, a vile stench assaulted Jessie's senses.

"Take a look at these fine specimens," Bull laughed.

Jessie peered across the room. Inside a large closet was a huge copper tub. In the tub were two naked men, bound and gagged.

"Got us a bounty hunter and a U.S. marshal, came here with big ideas. Look at 'em now, both of them, swimming in it," Bull said.

Bull glowered at the bounty hunter, then slid the closet door shut. He brushed past Barabbas, then plopped down in a divan. His meat hanging over the edge, he ordered a brunette, her body glittering in gold and diamonds, on her knees. She complied.

"What are you two drinkin'?" the barmaid called out.

"Whiskey. Bring a bottle," Jessie said.

"Allow me, Jane," a skinny guy with a crooked mouth and bad teeth told the barmaid.

The skinny guy plucked the bottle out of Jane's hands. He grinned at Jessie. He moved away from the bar. Two, then three of his cronies fell in behind him. Trouble.

"Oh, shit, here we go," Jessie muttered to Ki.

"Like the man said," Ki growled. "Welcome to Hell."

★

Chapter 4

From her core, Jessie felt rage and pain burning and expanding and consuming her. She was a bundle of emotional dynamite about to blow. These days, she knew she was constantly on edge, that violence had become an alluring thing for her, at once feeding her pain and easing it. It was time to ease her pain.

She didn't even acknowledge the presence of the leering foursome. She didn't have time for this shit. She didn't play the insult game, do the word dance, or throw around threats. Just a look and maybe as few words as possible, let them have what they thought was their moment to ride the thunder of their pride, then shatter their world and reduce them to dogshit.

"Here's your bottle, ma'am."

The grinner put the bottle on the table.

Jessie heaved a breath, told Ki, "Looks like testing time. Let's shoot for an A-plus."

One of them farted. The farter said, "Hell's that s'posed to mean? A-plus? A for asshole? That's what I see here, good-lookin' whore with some half-breed asshole."

One of them had a hard-on, and he was diddling with himself. "Like a taste, baby?" The boner-squeezer laughed. "Like what you see?"

With a sardonic grin, Jessie answered, "Funny, I don't see anything. But I bet I've seen a bigger pecker on a chicken."

Laughter erupted from Bull.

"Get up, bitch!" the fourth one, who had a runny nose, rasped.

Meanness hardened Jessie's face. She held Ki's grim stare for a stretched second, as Leaky Nose repeated his demand.

Jessie got up, all right. She drove a fist into the grinner's face. As he shrieked, Jessie slammed the whiskey bottle across his face, jagged pieces of glass spearing into his cheeks. Ki lashed out with a sweeping kick, clipping Leaky Nose in the back of his knee, dropping him on his back. Both Jessie and Ki leapt to their feet at the same instant. Ki pulped the farter's nose with the heel of his palm. There was blood and howling and men dancing in agony, with looks that said they'd surely bitten off much more than they could chew.

It was too late for mercy. Jessie showed them none. If anything, she turned it up a notch to go all the way.

A craning hook kick from Ki and the grinner

was lifted off his feet and hurled a good ten feet backward.

The bullwhip slipped off Jessie's shoulder. Boner-squeezer reached for his revolver, but the whip lashed his hand. As he screamed and clutched his hand, Jessie flung the whip again, and sent his revolver flying across the room. She launched a sideways kick into his crotch, driving him back, then she slashed his face then balls with the whip.

"Ahhh, you bitch!" Boner Squeezer roared.

Grinner stood.

The whip scorched the air. There was now howling laughter from the mob in the saloon, as the whip curled around the grinner's leg, and Jessie wrenched him off his feet. As he lay there, she began flaying his ass and back and shoulders. He cried in terror, tried to crab away from her on all fours. Jessie followed him, stinging him, told him, "You better learn the difference between a lady and a whore! You understand?"

Ki finished off the farter, the squeezer and the nose with a series of devastating punches and kicks, dropping them out cold in a heap.

Jessie kicked the grinner square in the ass as he tried to stand. The grinner tumbled through a card table, splintering it to pulp, scattering angry card players, one of them enraged because he had a winning hand and was on the verge of turning his luck. He kicked the grinner in the face.

Jessie stood, legs splayed over her victim. Blood streaming down his face, he looked up at her in pure terror.

37

Everyone held their breath, eyes, burning with fascination and hunger, locked on Jessie.

"Do you understand me?" Jessie growled.

"Y-yes—"

"Say it!"

"I understand."

"Apologize!"

The look of pride started to harden the grinner's eyes, so Jessie stung him again.

"Yes, yes! I'm sorry!"

Jessie turned, but kept one eye on her victim, heading back for her table. "Someone get me another bottle."

Barabbas, grinning in admiration, said, "Here."

The bounty hunter walked up to her and politely handed her a fresh bottle.

Groaning from Ki's victims broke the silence.

Bull suddenly roared with laughter, then clapped his hands, long and hard. "All of you, listen to me and listen good. Do not mess with these people again or you will have a problem you will not be able to handle. By God, I like these people, I like their style." More roaring laughter and clapping. "Anything they want, it's on the house."

"What?" the barmaid spat.

"You heard me. All right, I'll do this for you so you won't have a constant shit fit. They get free booze, food they pay for. And rooms. You got a problem with that?"

Jane scowled, then withered up in brooding silence.

Jessie sat as the four beaten men tried to clamber to their feet. They never made it.

It happened so fast, Jessie flinched in shock.

Without warning, Bull grabbed a revolver from one of the patrons of Hell. Swiftly, he walked up to the grinner, who screamed, "Noooo! Bull!"

Bull jammed the muzzle against his forehead, pulled the trigger, and blew his brains out.

The farter, the squeezer and the nose went down next. In panic, they tried to run for the door, but Bull dropped them with three quick shots, hammering them into each other, dropping them in a bloody pile on the floor.

Smoking gun in hand, Bull barked, "Somebody throw this shit out the door."

Bull pitched the gun away. Several of the whores laughed.

Jessie felt sick to her stomach all of a sudden. Their laughter and their evil became a distant thing to her, as she retreated into herself. She wanted to be alone.

She took a deep pull of whiskey.

As the day wore on, Jessie played cards with Ki. She kept an eye on the patrons of Hell, her ears primed for any hint that Billy Johnson was there. Barabbas sat at the bar, drinking and smoking, eventually ordering and digging into a huge slab of steak. No one bothered the three of them.

"Jessie, can I tell you something?"

Jessie stared at Ki's worried expression. "If you must."

Ki heaved a breath. "We need to do something, make a move. I don't like to see this happening to you. It scares me. Please understand my feelings."

"Ki, believe me when I tell you I understand your feelings all too well. Let it ride. But understand this much. These weeks of travelling have taken their toll. The evilness of this place is having its effect on me. I don't know that I'll be the same person when we leave here. Enough said."

Ki fell silent. He poured himself a shot of whiskey, killed it. "Can't beat 'em," he muttered, "join 'em."

So, wondering if she was just spiting Ki but not really caring, Jessie drank two straight shots, wanting to get drunk but fighting it so she could be ready for trouble, or a break in her hunt. *So many ghosts, so much pain*, she thought, feeling angrier and sorrier the meaner her buzz got. *How much more can I take?*

Toward evening, many of the whores went to rooms upstairs with their johns. Jessie was glad they left. You cannot sit in the presence of evil, she thought, without somehow being affected by it. Her own soul, troubled and perverse at times these days, hungered for something raw and dirty. Barabbas was her target.

The door opened, and what she assumed were regulars bellied up to the bar. They talked in low tones, wearing the look of the lost and lonely, their voices and their stories edged between self-pity, sarcasm, and self-loathing. They were older men in the final tired clinging phase of their lives, and she overheard them say they were unemployed, alone in the world with no family, no jobs, no money, and no hope, obviously just cronies who gathered together to drink and share their own personal misery. Jessie could tell they were not bad men, rather they were the good that is weak, meat, once good, now spoiling and ripe for the maggots. There was Tom the ex-judge. There was Rufus the ex-lawyer. There was Pete the ex-newspaperman, who talked about writing a great American novel, and who was chided for his constant drunkenness by Tom, who said he wouldn't amount to shit if he didn't put down the bottle, because how the hell could he do anything when he was always drinking himself into oblivion, then sleeping it off. Pete would retort with feeble defenses, then both Tom and Pete would lapse into brooding silence, or they might begin irritating people with their strange behavior. Almost everything Tom said had some borderline obscene or sexual insinuation. Meanwhile, Pete rambled on about alien beings from another planet, called them the Others, said they were supposed to be there soon.

Jane groaned, cursed, and only when she threatened to cut them off would they shut up. Minutes later, they started up again, then Jane threw in that she wanted a twenty-percent gratuity, plus time on the barstool, that their no-good, deadbeat, cheapskate asses were taking up space at her bar. So they shut up for another few minutes, and then it started all over again.

This little scene at the bar tired Jessie quickly. So she drank some more, and she found herself staring longer and harder at Barabbas. Strange thoughts danced through her mind.

Twice, she saw some of Bull's lackeys walk up to him while he was being stroked and sucked on the divan by one of the whores. They would say something to him, and Jessie saw Barabbas tense up, listening hard, trying to catch what they were saying.

After this happened a third time, Barabbas got off his barstool, was reminded by Jane he owed money, twenty percent plus time on the barstool. He paid, and announced the heavy tip he'd left for her. There was no thank-you from Jane, just a scowl and a curse.

Barabbas came over to Jessie and Ki. He looked over his shoulder to satisfy himself that no one was looking their way.

"He's here," Barabbas said. "They were talking about the kid. That's all I caught, just 'kid,' a couple of times. Heard Bull say take care of the kid, don't let him in here right now." Barabbas paused, Jessie staring him in the eye.

"Go order me a steak, one for Ki, too," Jessie told the bounty hunter. "Medium rare. Potatoes and a fresh bottle. Your treat, big spender."

Barabbas chuckled. He shrugged. "Sure. Anything you want."

"Anything?"

Barabbas gave her a hard look. "I'll take care of your dinners. Then I'm turning in for the night."

As he turned and walked away, Jessie felt Ki's stare boring into her.

"Don't say a thing, Ki."

"Wasn't going to."

"Good."

Jessie waited a full half hour for their steaks. She ate, she drank, she had a smoke. She stood.

Without looking at Ki, she took the bottle, her body and soul geared to target in on the bounty hunter named Barabbas. She stopped, turned, smiled at Ki, then picked up her whip.

"Forgot something," she told Ki.

★

Chapter 5

Having gotten his room number from Jane, Jessie, bottle in one hand, the whip in the other hand, walked down the long, narrow upstairs hall, her face hard, her eyes grim and determined, shining with their own wild light against the flickering glow of a lone kerosene lantern hung from the ceiling.

She came to his door and knocked.

"Yeah?"

"Open up," she told Barabbas. "It's me."

He opened the door, stood there, his eyes bleary, his body swaying slightly, a half-empty bottle in his hand. His smile was mean.

"You are positively the most ugly man I have ever seen in my life," she said. "There is not one single thing I find attractive about you."

He looked at the whip, then his grin widened.

45

"Thank you, kind lady, that's the nicest thing I've heard in some time."

"You're welcome," she said, and shouldered her way past him. "Close the door."

He did. She moved into the light of his kerosene lamp.

"What's the whip for?"

She gave him a twisted smile. "Let me ask you something. Do you consider me a whore?"

He shrugged. "No."

"You hesitate."

"You're a lady. And a whore. There's a fine line."

"But I'm white."

"Whatever that means. Oh, I get it, the tale of the boots and the Indian's white whore. Look, I've had all kinds of women, what and who they are doesn't really mean a damn thing to me. Just another hole."

"I see. I knew that already, though."

He sucked on his bottle, sat down on the edge of the bed, rolled a cigarette, fired up.

"You're lookin' at me like you want to know somethin', lady."

"I know enough."

"You don't know shit. See, that's the problem with the world. Everyone thinks they know somethin' when they don't even know themselves. What you don't understand is that most people are garbage and deserve to be treated just like that."

"Ugly outside, ugly inside."

Barabbas laughed. "It's called the process of life. And spare me the who-are-you-really routine. I come from nothing, I have no family, no friends. No past, no real trauma or tragedy for me, and, no, my real name is not Barabbas. I ride, I kill, I make money. I go my own way. I drink, I smoke, I bed whoever comes along."

"So bed me."

He cocked an eyebrow.

"Or do you have no use for a white whore?"

"Oh, shit."

She took off her clothes, but left her boots on.

Now Barabbas was checking out the full package with careful and eager inspection. He swallowed hard.

"Damn," was all he said.

Jessie smiled. "Don't think you can just take what you want, either."

"Never. I've seen you in action. Hey, I got respect for the right woman."

Seconds dragged out, as Barabbas sat there, mesmerized by her stunning naked beauty.

"Games?" Barabbas said.

"Why not? Everyone else plays them here. When among the savages—"

She saw the bulge in his pants.

"I want you to take off your clothes and get on your knees," she told him.

"Okay, okay," he said, then shed his clothes.

"Understand, I don't want you, but I'm taking you on my terms and my terms only. Do you understand me?"

He went along. Funny, the new Jessie thought, what a painful hard-on in the presence of a beautiful woman can do to a man.

47

"On your knees."

Barabbas knelt.

"Turn around. Put your nose on the floor."

He did.

Jessie's blood rushed hot, and she felt the sticky moisture flow between her legs. Here was this man, tough guy, cold-blooded killer, being reduced to a groveling worshipping worm before her feet. Perversion worked in her mind and excited her, and this was not the first time, either, where her fantasy and warped desires became reality. There were no limits to what Jessie's mind could conjure, no limits to what her heart could desire. Perversion and pure lust sated is degrading and ugly, and it leaves you feeling stained and ashamed, Jessie knew. It makes you want to hide in the dark, flee yourself. But, what the hell, she decided, she was up for ugly and degrading. Later, she could flee and hide and despise herself.

"Turn around."

He turned on his knees. Jessie stood over him, lifted one leg, set her foot down on the edge of the bed.

She shivered as he put his lips on her sopping wetness. She held him by the back of his head, holding him in his place. She moaned, smiled, laughed.

"Lick, that's right, just lick," she cried.

Within seconds, she cried out, shivering in orgasm.

Then she turned around, and he ran his mouth with light pecking kisses over her buttocks. She spread her cheeks, made him lick her, long and deep, grinding her ass into his face. Finally, laughing, she wheeled around and slapped his face hard. He growled, looked set to explode with anger.

"Don't you dare, you stay on your knees until I tell you to get up. I control you, I own you, both your body and your soul."

She sat down on the edge of the bed and opened her legs. "Crawl to me on your knees."

When she had him in position, she made him kiss her, from her feet, all the way up her legs, then lick her to yet another orgasm.

"Damn it, lady, you're making me crazy."

Jessie laughed, tossed her blonde mane around. She rolled onto the bed, on her hands and knees. "I don't want to look at your ugly face."

"Fine with me."

She cried out, as he speared her from behind, going in fast and deep and rough. She could feel him on the verge of shooting, him, wanting to get it over with fast.

She pulled away, and he cursed, his heavy meat slapping up against his belly.

"What the hell—"

Jessie rolled onto her back. "I changed my mind. I want to see your ugly face, after all."

She spread her legs, but this time took him in her hand, stroking him, squeezing him hard, her hand sliding down, then cupping his sac. She squeezed him hard, making him squirm, a strangled cry of pain locked in his throat, his eyes bulging. Jessie laughed at his discomfort, telling him she could have him anytime she wanted, if she wanted, and did he understand. Yes, he did.

She pulled her legs back, guiding him into her. She let him pump her for a few seconds, then fisted his balls again, squeezing. With her other hand, she slapped his face, lifted a leg, planted her foot on his face and pushed him away. Then she reached down, began stroking him with a fury, his cock pulsing and hot in her hand.

"What the hell are you doing, lady?"

She laughed, her wild-eyed gaze on his pole. She kept stroking until he squirted. He moaned and writhed. When the final spurt was over, she released him.

"What the hell you keep laughing for?"

"I need some sleep," Jessie said.

"You're crazy, you know that."

"No crazier than you or anybody else."

Jessie turned her back to him. She was exhausted, and it felt good to crawl beneath the blanket, warm and satisfied.

Barabbas's snoring woke her up. At first, nothing seemed real to Jessie. She was sickened by what she had done with a man she felt nothing but contempt for. But, maybe, she told herself, it was just what she had needed. Either way, she felt meaner and harder and colder than before. She looked at Barabbas in the lamplight, his mouth open, as he snored away in drunken exhaustion. He was a disgusting sight, lying there, snoring away, naked and sated and feeling good. An idea came to her mind. She needed to make a point.

She rolled out of bed, still in her boots. She strapped on her gun belt. Naked except for her holster, she straddled his chest, rubbing herself on him. He stirred, groaned, smacked his lips. He was like an animal, a sick animal she felt compelled to put to sleep for good. The animal does not understand nor does it care what it does, she thought, it only lives to hunt and kill, eat and procreate. That summed up for her exactly all Barabbas was to her and to the world. If she killed him tomorrow, she would feel nothing. So what did that make her? An animal, also? Perhaps.

Suddenly, she drew her revolver, jammed the muzzle in his mouth.

Barabbas woke abruptly, his eyes wide with fear as Jessie cocked the hammer.

"You listen to me, mister. Listen good. Do not betray me. I'm talking about the kid. If you harm him, I will kill you. Nod if you understand."

He nodded carefully.

Jessie laughed. "Good. I'm feeling horny again. What you are to me, is my lick-boy, my licking dog, nothing more. That's all. You'll never have or know all of me. I want you to know that, I want you to be tormented by that. I want you to see my sweet ass in your mind, my sweet tender pussy in your dreams, my wet mouth, know that you will never know the pleasure of having them. You will think and you will lust for me, fully aware that you will not have me—ever again. Now, this is what we do," she breathed, mashing herself on the hard muscles of his stomach. "I keep this gun in your mouth. Gently, you spread my ass."

Slowly, carefully, she uncocked the hammer, his

cry of fear muted by the muzzle jammed down his throat.

She felt his hands, sweating and trembling, on her ass, kneading her cheeks, spreading them apart. She writhed and moaned, grinding herself into him, the gun staying rammed in his mouth. A full two minutes later, orgasm ripped through her. For long moments, sweating and shaking, she remained on top of him. Finally, she slipped the gun out of his mouth, wiped his slobber on the muzzle off on his pillow, then holstered her gun.

"Thanks, I needed that," she told him.

With cold anger in his eyes, he said, "That was not a smart thing to do."

She showed him a strange smile, rolled off him. "I know. I don't care."

"You better start caring. Like I said, the games are over."

"Meaning, I'm back to being a whore again?"

"Call it what you want. Don't ever do something like that again."

"Go back to sleep. Remember what I said."

She left the room, wanting to be alone, wanting to flee and hide, but hungry for confrontation to ease her pain. Still naked except for the holster and her boots and the bullwhip curled around her shoulder, she moved down the hall. She heard snoring all around her. A figure appeared at the foot of the steps. The shadow staggered, a bottle in hand. It came toward her as she descended the steps. The man didn't even look at her as he stumbled past. At the top of the steps, the man collapsed in a drunken stupor.

Jessie moved into the saloon. She looked around, the room lit in gloomy shadows by one kerosene lantern. Except for three men nodding off or snoring away by the closet, there was no one there. Slowly, she walked toward the closet, intending right then to free the captive U.S. marshal. It would create a stir, and it was dangerous, but she felt free and strong and ready and willing to take on anybody and everybody.

As she stood before the men in the saloon, she smiled and laughed to herself. She gave the place one last look. She stepped back, then hammered a powerful kick off a bearded jaw, dropping that guy to the floor in a heap, blood pouring from his shattered mouth. She kicked the next guy square in the jaw, snapping teeth and jawbone. The man toppled, and the third one groaned, waking up. His eyes began to open, but Jessie drilled the toe of her boot square in his balls, shutting those eyes of bulging agony, then she dropped him, also, with a kick to the jaw.

She moved to the bar, found rope. Quickly, she undressed the three men, tying them together. Sucking in a deep breath, she opened the closet door. Jessie grabbed a knife from one of the felled drunks. She cut the rope off the hands of one of the men in the closet.

"Say nothing, not a word. Get dressed and leave and do not return here. Make a sound, I will tie you back up and leave you here."

The guy pulled the gag out of his mouth, began choking, sucking air.

"Quiet," Jessie hissed.

53

"Lady, I'm a U.S. marshal. I'll be damned if I let this go unpunished. This is an abomination! I will not let this go. I will return!"

"Then you, sir, are one very stupid man."

She walked away, but not before saying, "You create any noise, you do not head straight for the door, I will shoot you in the legs and tell Bull you were trying to escape."

"I'll remember this, lady, and you'll pay, too," the marshal said.

Silently, Jessie walked to the bar. There, as the marshal dressed, croaking and choking on his stink, Jessie poured herself a shot of whiskey. Out of the corner of her eye, she watched and waited until the marshal had dressed and left.

Then a voice said, "Nice work. Nice body, too. Bad smell, though."

She wheeled, searching the gloom. He stood, stepped from the far shadows of the saloon. Jessie drew her gun.

"What, you going to shoot me in cold blood and wake the whole place up? I don't think Bull would think too kindly of you letting his shit-suckers go like that."

"Who are you?"

The guy was tall, bearded, and long-haired, dressed in a long white coat. "Name's not important. I'm leaving anyway," he said, raking Jessie up and down with a leer. He whistled softly. "You are one beautiful woman."

Jessie just glared at him.

"Tough, too."

"Get out of here."

"Sure. But be warned."

Jessie kept her Colt trained on the tall shadow. "About what?"

"What it is, I'm doing a little recon for the general. Hell is about to burn. Good night, ma'am."

With that, the tall shadow left the saloon. For long moments, uncertain of his intentions, feeling afraid and alone, she stared at the doorway. She holstered her gun. Then Jessie dragged the unconscious men inside the closet, shut the door, leaving them in the dark and the stink.

Tomorrow should prove most interesting, she thought.

★
Chapter 6

Tomorrow proved most interesting indeed.

The sun had risen high over Apocalypse, but it was difficult for Jessie to tell how late in the morning it was, for the mist remained, heavy and thick, an impenetrable white shroud wrapping the town. Jessie, having just bathed and dressed, was looking out the window. She was in Barabbas's room, but the bounty hunter was gone. Where he'd gone, she didn't know, didn't care.

"One day older, while the world grows colder," she said to herself. "Can you feel the worms?"

There was a knock on the door.

She opened the door, found Ki outside.

"Good morning," he said, looking at her, every bit as uncertain and anxious as yesterday.

"Is it?" Jessie muttered. "Let's go eat."

With her gun strapped to her hip, she headed downstairs. "What time is it?"

57

"Almost noon. Slept late. Tired, were you?"

She snorted. "And sick." It was quiet down there in the saloon, too quiet.

They found them all gathered in the saloon. Bull was sitting in his usual spot, naked and half-drunk by now, his blonde whore on her knees before him, her face and hungry mouth never too far from him. Jessie and Ki stopped in the middle of the room. Something felt wrong, and Jessie read Bull's look of amused suspicion.

"Ah, there you are, beautiful lady," Bull greeted, stood, and shoved his whore away. Swaying, bottle in hand, he walked toward Jessie and Ki. "Sleeping late, were you? Not sick, are you, beautiful?"

Everybody's worried about my health, how touching, Jessie thought. She searched the room and found Barabbas at the table she and Ki had occupied yesterday. He was drinking and cutting up a big steak. He looked at her, and Jessie met his stare. There was anger in his eyes, and she detected just a hint of shame. Good. She wanted him to feel used and cheap and humiliated. Nice going, Jess, she thought and smiled to herself.

"Got me something of a big pre-dick-a-ment here," Bull said. He brushed past Jessie and Ki, chuckling, opening the closet. Sharing the tub with the bounty hunter were the three men Jessie had clobbered last night. They were bound and gagged. Bull pulled the gag from one of their mouths.

"Please, Bull, please, let me out! I didn't do nothin', Bull! This ain't fair!"

"Life ain't fair, boy. You were supposed to be watching them. You messed up, so, what am I supposed to do? Just let it ride? Then what? I look weak. I can't look weak, or I lose respect."

"Come on, Bull—"

Bull jammed the gag back in the guy's mouth and shut the closet door. He walked up to Jessie and Ki. He stood there, looming over them, smiling.

"What do you think?" Bull said, then downed a slug of whiskey. "What I think, we have ghosts in the building. Last night, these ghosts, they came through here and set that marshal free, then these ghosts, they vanish into the night. I hate ghosts. Makes Bull nervous. When I get nervous—well, there's no telling what I'll do. So, I see any ghosts tonight or any other time—" He forced a shudder. "Scary stuff. Ghosts. Watch out for the ghosts."

With a strange laugh, Bull stepped past them and assumed his position on the divan.

"Breakfast's on me," Bull announced. "Whatever they want, Jane. Okay with you, beautiful?"

"What'll I owe you?" Jessie called out, grinning.

Bull just laughed. "By God, I like your style."

"Never met a man who didn't," Jessie laughed back.

Bull howled with laughter. "You don't owe me a thing but the pleasure of allowing me to feast my eyes on your beauty."

"I'm flattered, kind sir."

"Pleasure's all mine, most gorgeous one. And, no, you flatter us by just being here."

So the Gorgeous One and Ki sat with Barabbas. Barabbas didn't look up, kept shoveling steak and potatoes into his mouth.

"Any plans for today?" the bounty hunter finally said.

Jessie ignored him, ordered herself a steak with potatoes and bread. She ordered a fresh bottle and put the whiskey on Barabbas's tab. The bounty hunter didn't object. Ki declined to eat and busied himself with a game of solitaire.

When Jessie was finished with her meal, she fired up a smoke, blew a cloud in the bounty hunter's face, and said, "You ever hear of the general?"

Barabbas tensed up, looked at Jessie for the first time since she'd sat down. "Why?"

"Answer my question."

Ki listened, looking worried and intense.

"Yeah. They call him—" Barabbas scanned the room for eavesdroppers, but the day's festivities in Hell were under way, the usual drinking, gambling, and open fornicating. "They call him General Misery," the bounty hunter continued. "And for good reason. Confederate soldier. Was a colonel, actually. Got a whole slew of real bad boys riding with him. They've been on the run for years, still living out the war they lost. Anyone's fair game. The usual stuff: rape, torture, murder. There's a fifty thousand dollar bounty on his head, five hundred apiece for any of the other shit riding with him. Now, you answer me. Why do ask about him?"

"Like stud said—ghosts. I saw ghosts last night." Jessie smiled. "One of these ghosts, he was here. Got up, told me he was doing a little recon for this general. Said Hell will burn."

Barabbas cursed. "If they ride through here, Hell will burn."

"We need to make a move, Jess," Ki said. "I don't want to keep playing the waiting game."

Jessie looked at Barabbas. Despite the fear in the bounty hunter's eyes, she could almost see him dreaming of fifty big ones. Five apiece for each of the rest of the bags of shit.

"You could be a rich man," Jessie said.

"Yeah. If I live to spend it."

Jessie grunted, fell silent. She smoked and drank and played poker with Ki. Several hours passed, then Ki repeated that they needed to make a move.

"Tonight, Ki," Jessie told him. "Tonight we go in search of ghosts. If he's here, we'll find him."

Jessie slowly got drunk. She looked across the room, found Bull nodding off. "Bull? Bull!?"

Bull snapped awake. "Ma'am?"

"You're so polite," Jessie said with a wry grin. "That's one of the things I really like about you."

"Yes, ma'am. And only one of the things?" He chuckled. "Please, go on. You have my undivided interest."

"Easy, Bull, don't get all excited. Stay polite," Jessie said in a soft but warning voice.

"Me, I'm always polite, ma'am, I even always say please and thank you, even to my whores. Even before I kill a man. What can I do for you, ma'am?"

"Just a fresh bottle."

"Jane. Get movin'. You heard the lady. Put it on your buddy's tab, or you want Bull should buy this one?"

"You can buy this one."

"Very good."

Scowling, with begrudging effort, Jane brought a bottle over to Jessie's table, slammed it down, cursed, then skulked off.

The Painter walked into Hell about an hour later. Everyone seemed excited by his arrival. Jessie watched as one of Bull's whores set up an easel and got some brushes and paint.

"How are we doing today, Painter?" Bull asked. "Feel inspired?"

The Painter shrugged. Jessie looked at him closely. At one time, he was perhaps a good-looking man, but it was hard to tell, it was even hard to determine his age. He was gray and gaunt, skinny and stoop-shouldered and white-haired now, with a full white beard that seemed to pull his head forward. He smoked and sucked from a bottle of whiskey. He hacked and trembled, and it seemed it was all he could do to walk across the room toward the easel.

"Kidneys actin' up on you again, Painter? Take it easy on the whiskey, okay? Please."

Jessie couldn't believe it, Bull actually looked concerned about The Painter. Without a word, one of the whores placed a stool in front of the easel. She actually looked at The Painter with reverence in her eyes. She took him by the shoulders and helped him sit. Gently, she kissed him once on the cheek. Then she took a full minute to massage his shoulders and arms. There was nothing sexual in the way she rubbed him down; it was obvious this was some sort of ritual. The Painter was something of an idol, a god to them all.

"Comfortable, Painter? Hey, you want somethin' to eat, Painter?" Bull asked in a tender voice. "Come on, you should eat somethin'. I worry about you."

"No. But thank you. I'm fine."

The Painter spoke slowly, softly. His expression seemed carved into a perpetual grim and troubled look, his eyes haunted and full of sorrow. One of the whores dressed him in a white smock and handed him a brush.

"Do you need somethin' real quick, Painter?" Bull asked, still concerned, still gentle. "Get you anything?"

"If you mean sex, no, thank you."

"I understand, Painter. Kills the creative drive. Okay, what will it be today?"

"You pick it, kind sir."

Jessie watched, fascinated by The Painter. He just sat there, so withered, so still, his haunted stare so locked on the blank canvas, it was as if he might be searching for his own soul somewhere in the nothingness before him. Who was this man? He seemed so alone, so disturbed, Jessie felt some overwhelming compulsion to take him in her arms and hold him like a mother would a baby. He took a deep pull of whiskey, then Bull snapped his fingers and one of his whores gently took the bottle from The Painter's hands. The man didn't protest. He fired up a cigarette, and the whore set a stand beside him with an ashtray on it. Violently, The Painter coughed for several moments. Everyone watched him closely, waiting on him, silently, respectfully giving him all the time he needed to get composed. After his third cigarette, he quieted down. He asked Bull for one more shot of whiskey. Bull was quiet for a long moment, deciding, then relented.

"Just one more, Painter, that's it. Please? Don't start bugging me about that. Please. I kindly implore you to give it a rest."

The Painter nodded. "Fine. Whatever you say. Just one more, I'll let it be then."

So The Painter got his last drink before getting to work. It would be the first and the last time Jessie ever saw him smile. It was the rebellious smile of a child, happy at getting his way.

Bull barked at one of the men at the bar. "You, I need a volunteer!"

The guy slowly turned with a scared look.

"Yeah, you! Get your clothes off, asshole. Now! Stacey! Take charge of this asshole, baby!"

The redheaded whipmistress, naked but for her black leather boots, wrapped her whip around the volunteer's throat and hauled him off his stool.

"You heard the man," she snarled in the guy's bulging eyes. She kept the whip wrapped around his neck, as he shed his clothes. She pulled the guy along, flung him down in front of the easel.

"On your ass!" she ordered the guy.

The guy whimpered, but rolled over. Stacey ground her boot against his throat, laughed.

"Keep that look on your face. That's right, my little ass-licker! I want to see nothing but pain and shame. Relax, asswipe, you're going to be made immortal in Hell. Me and you, forever."

It didn't take much effort to hold that look of pain and shame.

The Painter got busy. His brush moved with a fury, so fast his hand was a blur. Once in awhile, he might glance at his subjects, but he seemed to be able to just paint them from his mind's eye. Jessie watched, at once fascinated by The Painter's obvious talent, and sickened at the sight of what he had to paint.

Stacey stood there, her whip hanging by her long, firm, shapely, ivory-white leg, the other hand on her hip, staring down at her worm with arrogance and contempt.

And so The Painter painted and chain-smoked, unmindful of all the ashes he scattered everywhere, missing the ashtray altogether. "Would you kindly ask him to turn his face, just a little toward me?" The Painter said in his soft voice. "Just a little, not much, please, if you would?"

Stacey barked at the guy to turn his face a little. Gagging, the guy did what he was told.

The saloon was filled with an awed and reverent silence as The Painter worked. It didn't take long before Jessie witnessed the man's incredible talent. He painted Stacey and her subject with raw and haunting lifelike detail, caught their expressions perfectly, brought them to life on the canvas, so real, so three-dimensional, it was almost impossible to distinguish reality from the painting.

Perhaps it was several hours later, but Jessie couldn't tell because she was so mesmerized by the sight of what she could only describe as divine talent.

The Painter announced that he was finished. They gathered around and whistled softly, admiring the painting. Stacey smiled at the picture of herself, her eyes gleaming with awe.

"God, that is beautiful," Stacey breathed, her firm, melon-sized breasts just inches from The Painter's face, the whipmistress looking set to cry with pride and joy. "You are amazing, Painter. God, I wish you would take me and fuck me forever."

The Painter said nothing, his expression unchanged.

The other subject of the painting spent long moments just gagging, sucking wind, rubbing his throat.

"You ass!" Stacey snarled at the guy. "Stay where you are. I'm not finished with you!" With hunger, she looked at The Painter. "Painter, please, just one night, you'll never forget it. I beg you."

"That's very kind of you," The Painter said, without looking at her. "But, no, thank you."

"Hey, leave The Painter alone," Bull growled at Stacey. "I don't want his talent stained by the likes of you. Okay, how much, Painter?"

"Nothing. You know that."

"Come on, Painter," Bull said, an edge to his voice. "Damn it, man, you got talent like I never seen. You never take my money. I don't get you."

"No money, kind sir. Please understand."

Bull heaved a breath. "I tell ya what, Painter, if Bull didn't like you so much, he would be insulted. How about a nice steak at least?"

"No. I'm not hungry. I'm tired. I feel sad and alone. I need rest."

"All right, all right. Whatever you want, Painter, you know that."

"Would one of your ladies walk me back to my room?"

"Donna, you go with him," Bull ordered a blonde. "You know the routine. Sit with him for awhile, hold his hand, and talk to him."

Donna didn't look too happy about this.

"Look, slut, you wipe that frown off your face or I'll slap it off you, you understand me!"

"Dammit, Bull," Donna whined. "I always get stuck taking him back to his room. It's scary. He just lays there in bed, naked and diddlin' with himself, he can barely get hard, he's so drunk, then I gotta use my mouth. Talkin' strange stuff, just starin' at the ceiling. Last time, you know what he says? He says, 'Dear God, forgive me my sins, do you not hear me? Do you not feel what I feel? Is there anybody out there?' And, last time, get this, I didn't tell ya this. You know what he does? He takes a shit, right in the middle of the floor, then—then he asks me to wipe him."

"Did you?" one of the men chuckled.

"I was too damn scared not to!" Donna rasped, to an outburst of fresh laughter. "Bull, I ain't goin' this time! I ain't goin'!"

Bull gritted his teeth. "You stupid, ungrateful whore, you'll go and you'll like it. He wants you to suck him, you'll do it and you'll like it. He wants his ass wiped, you'll wipe it and you'll wipe it good and clean and you'll like it. You understand me? You want a beating like you've never had?"

"May I leave now, kind sir?" The Painter asked.

Bull glared at Donna. She scowled and cursed. Bull backhanded her once, then she helped The Painter to stand.

"My bottle, please."

Bull himself handed The Painter a fresh bottle.

"Good night," the Painter said.

"Tomorrow, Painter?" Bull asked. Donna, bleeding from the mouth but holding The Painter by the shoulders, guided him to the door. "Painter?"

"I don't know. I'll see how I feel. If I don't feel up to it—please, forgive me."

"Take care of him, Donna!" Bull warned. "If I have to send someone to check up on you—"

"All right, all right!" Donna whined.

"Kind sir," The Painter said to no one in particular. "Forgive me if you do not see me for a few days. I really don't feel well, I feel especially— disturbed."

Bull looked frightened. "Okay, okay, whatever you want, Painter. Get some rest, all right. And, please, go easy on the firewater. I'll keep an eye on you, don't you worry. You are the man."

"Jesus," Barabbas muttered as they admired the Painter's latest effort. "Pathetic. Weird, too. Goddamn weirdo."

Jessie glared at the bounty hunter. "You know something, I'd be disappointed if you didn't feel that way."

"Guy's a nut," Barabbas insisted, but in a low voice. "Stud was practically tripping over his cock to baby the guy. Pathetic."

Jessie shook her head.

Stacey dragged her subject, her whip wrapped around his throat, into a back room. Moments later, the sound of her whip lashing his flesh and his cries of torment filled the saloon.

Ki heaved a breath, and Jessie looked him in the eye.

"What?" Jessie said.

"I don't know, Jessie," Ki said, looking troubled as usual. "I need some fresh air. I'll be gone the rest of the day, but I'll be back."

Jessie showed Ki a knowing smile. "Have fun."

"I wish you meant that."

"Oh, but I do."

★

Chapter 7

His heart breaking, Ki rode hard through the mist. When he was far away from Apocalypse, he reined his mount in, bellowed at the sky. He thought he might throw up, was on the verge of puking, started to vomit, then gritted his teeth and swallowed.

What had happened to Jessie? Had he not ridden away when he did, he knew he would have said or done something that would do irreparable damage to their relationship. There was a wall between them, had been for some time, and it was killing him inside. Never had he seen her sleep with a man she would just as soon kill as look at. Of course, he hadn't seen her sleep with Barabbas, but he knew she'd spent the night in the bounty hunter's room, had seen the hunger in her eyes for the guy earlier, that strange light of defiance and recklessness that he had seen in her eyes for a long time now.

It was so sad and so very sickening. What, he asked himself, would turn it around? Somehow, some way, this venture into the town of evil must end with some good, or he feared there would be a point of no return, that crossing over where he would lose Jessie forever. He would rather she die than continue to live on the edge, teeth even bared at him, ready to jump at him.

Ki rode hard, stupidly taking his anger out on his horse, chancing a fall and breaking the horse's leg. Whether it was the mist, his mind, his emotions, or some fusing of the three, he didn't know, but he seemed to glide atop his horse through the wall of white. It was as if he was being pulled, harder and faster into the blinding white shroud. He roughly knew the distance to her cabin, and it should've been night when he arrived, but it wasn't. It was eerie and it was frightening. Time and distance suddenly had no semblance of reality. Perhaps it was night, he didn't know, couldn't tell.

Her cabin boiled at him through the mist.

She stood there, exactly where they had first seen her, in front of her black pot.

She turned her sightless eyes toward him.

He pulled his mount up in front of her, the horse heaving, on the verge of collapse.

"I know why you came back," Cassandra said, but she neither looked nor sounded pleased. In fact, she sounded angry to Ki. "You are full of fear and worry for the woman. I feel in you a terrible hunger to know the future. Let me say this to you, Ki. It is wrong for any man to know what the future holds. At times, yes, I can see the future, but I never tell the seeker of the future what is beyond today. It is wrong. It goes against nature, it goes against the will of God. However— come inside, sit with me awhile, I will know what to do later but only through your presence. I have already made some broth for you. I knew you would return. Come."

Ki dismounted and followed the blind woman toward her cabin.

She stopped suddenly and turned her blind eyes to him. "Understand this before entering my home. If you come here seeking to know all, then, my friend Ki, you shall leave here knowing nothing. Indeed, you will know far less than before. In my power there are hidden secrets. Once unleashed, they have a life of their own. They can steal a man's soul, his mind, and all of his memory. My only warning to you is this: Free yourself of hunger and desire and fear and worry. You must be like a child, innocent, with faith your only friend. Do not be afraid, because I care for you, because I sense in you basic good, I will help you free yourself. But you must trust me. Can you do this?"

For just a second, Ki hesitated. "I will try."

"You will do more than try. Your life and your soul, and the life and the soul of the woman you care about more than anything in this world hang in the balance of everything, in all that was, is, and will be. You see, I will tell you a secret. Eternity is all around us. The past, the present, and the future are as one. This is how eternity exists. It is with this knowledge alone that I can be helped to see the future, so that I can help you. The mind of man cannot grasp this concept, the hearts of men, because of fear and pride and desire for things of this world, blind them to the truth. It is all so simple, but that is the beauty of truth. Truth is simple and it is pure. Now. Follow me inside, but beware: You must become like a child. If you cannot, then you must leave here."

She left Ki standing there alone for a long and terrible moment. Again, Ki hesitated, then followed the blind woman into her home.

What Jessie had come to think of as the happy hour crowd arrived in Hell toward evening. One by one, Tom, Rufus, and Pete bellied up the bar to begin their usual song and dance, wondering where it had all gone and why. There were three new additions. There was Jason, who talked a lot about his cats and his dogs and his birds, who was every bit as lonely and pathetic as his cronies. There was the one-armed, one-eyed soldier, Benny, who had fought for the North, who drank whiskey fast and hard, and who became belligerent and combative almost right away. Finally, there was Bernie, the ex-tax collector from back East whose wife had left him for, of all things, another woman, a former slave named Jemima. Bernie was a sullen, brooding man who didn't say much. The others cruelly taunted him about his wife leaving him for a black woman. Tom, grinning, bottle of whiskey in hand, jeered, "Would it have made you feel better if she'd left ya for a black man instead?" Rufus added, "Maybe she did, she just didn't tell him."

The other patrons in Hell would just grin and chuckle at the regulars, occasionally throwing in their own cruel or sarcastic comments. Jessie watched and listened, feeling nothing for these regulars. They were pitiful losers. But they were accepted, sort of, by the gunmen. After all, they were all men, alone in their misery, sitting on the edge in the final tired clinging phase of their lives. The only difference between the gunmen and the regular alcoholics was that the gunmen lived for gold and blood, whereas the alcoholics lived in the past with no hope for the future. They lived only for the next drink, picking on each other to make themselves feel better about their pitiful state.

Jessie was now alone at her table. Minutes ago, a brooding Barabbas had said to her, "If you go looking for ghosts, I hope I'm invited."

To which Jessie had told him, "I'll let you know."

She probably would allow the bounty hunter to tag along when she and Ki searched the town for Billy Johnson, if only to keep an eye on Barabbas.

For some time, now, Jessie noticed Bull just sitting on his divan, brooding and silent. Whatever was eating him, he looked terribly disturbed. Finally, Bull bellowed at one of his whores, a comely redhead. "Rachel! Get your ass dressed and go check on Donna. I don't trust that bitch.

Dammit!" He paused, scowling. "I'm worried about The Painter. He doesn't look good. Guy doesn't eat, doesn't sleep. He doesn't take care of himself. Dammit! I tell ya what—if something happens to The Painter, I'll never be the same man again. It would be awful—awful for the world to lose genius like that. Get moving, whore!" he barked at Rachel, who, like Donna, didn't seem too pleased to have to baby-sit The Painter.

The Painter's latest effort had been hung on the closet door. Stacey sat before her image, admiring herself, drinking whiskey, and exclaiming, "God, it's beautiful!"

"Shut the hell up!" Bull flung back. "I got real problems here, I got real worries, bigger things to think about than your vanity. I got The Painter on my mind! Can't you see, can't you feel for anybody else other than yourself, whore? Damn your black, deceitful vile white whore's heart! You think you're something special? You only lust for money! You're disgusting!" Bull leapt to his feet, raced to the bar, grabbed a fresh bottle, then screamed at the whole room, "God damn you all! You're not even worth killing! You're useless, you're nothing, you do nothing, you say nothing, your lives mean nothing! God damn you!" Everyone fell silent in terror. "Assholes at the bar, look at these guys, look at these useless miserable bastards! Come in here, drink my whiskey, cheat my bartender! You, Mister Writer, you talk about writing this big book! You ain't shit! I got real talent, real genius across the street! You hear me? None of you are even worth shooting!" Bull stormed off to his room. "Assholes! Sluts! Something happens to The Painter—" He opened then slammed the door to his room behind the bar.

For what felt like an eternity, the whole saloon was silent, before Benny, the mutilated soldier, quietly growled, "I know he wasn't talking to me. Not me. I was in the War, I faced it down like a man. I was a hero. Nothin', huh? I'll show somebody nothin'. I know he wasn't talking to me."

Jessie heaved a breath, then shook her head.

Then Preacher Bob John arrived, and he was most certainly not received with the same warmth and reverence as The Painter. In fact, the short, fat, bald guy in the black outfit was greeted with groans and muttered cursing and contempt.

"You vile filth, you vermin, you who are full of Satan's desire, you who speak with the Devil's tongue!" Preacher Bob John railed at the people in the saloon. "How dare you mock a man of God!"

Some of the men laughed, some of them cursed, but all appeared somewhat tolerant of the preacher, sitting in their contemptuous silence. Another ritual.

The preacher leveled a menacing stare on every face in the room. "I warned you before, the evil you committed on the good people of this town will not go unpunished. You will pay! You will pay before man with your lives, then you will be judged before God and you will pay with your immortal souls! None of you evil creatures even had the decency to bury the good people of this town! You lie and you steal, you fornicate in the open, you murder, you rape—you shall all perish in the fires of Hell!"

"How 'bout I buy you a drink, preacher?" Rufus offered. "It might calm you down. I don't think anybody's in the mood for your crap."

"Crap!" the preacher roared. "Crap? How dare you. You call the word of God coming from a man of God, crap? You are truly beyond any hope, beyond any redemption." He sneered. "Yes, I see you, fat and lazy and strong in your pride, in your sin. All of you! I wait for the day when you go down in blood and fire. That day will come. I stay in this abomination you call Apocalypse only because I wish to see the day when you burn. And you will burn! Burn, burn, burn!"

Without another word, the preacher wheeled and stormed out of Hell.

Glad that was over, Jessie waited for night to come.

Jessie sensed a dangerous situation developing at the bar. Jane looked especially mean and threatening as the happy hour dragged on, and the whining and the mean-spirited bantering picked up a few notches. Perhaps it was both the whining and the fact that two of her regulars, Tom and the ex-taxman, nursed one beer for a full hour that made her expression dark with murderous intent. Naturally, she pointed out that she was not happy with them.

"You cheap bastards!" she told them. "I put up with this every stinking day. One beer, maybe two. You come in here, sit for three, sometimes four hours. Like Bull said before, only I'll add to that. Not only are you nothing, but you're taking up space at my bar. So this is it, I've had enough. This time, you leave a nice tip, plus money for time on the barstool. Got me?"

Bernie didn't get it. "What? Time on the barstool? You gotta be kidding."

Jane leaned up close to Bernie. "You see me laughing?"

"Time on the barstool?" Bernie repeated, bewildered as all hell. "I've never heard of such a thing. I've been drinking in bars for forty years, my money's good and this is got to be a first. Time on the barstool?"

"Which part didn't you understand?"

"The whole part. Time on the barstool?"

Jane heaved a breath, shut her eyes, muttered a curse. She was a barmaid on the edge.

"I don't get it," Bernie whined on. "Time on the barstool? What did I do? What did I do to make everyone so mad?"

"It's this!" Jane screamed. Without warning, the double-barreled shotgun swept up in Jane's hands. The barrels erupted smoke and flame and thunder, tunneled open his chest, and flung him halfway across the room.

Jessie couldn't believe her eyes at first, but, then again, nothing here surprised her anymore.

Cold silence descended over the room, the pure silence of terror and shock.

Not even blinking, Jane jacked open the shotgun, thrust two fresh cartridges into her smoking cannon. "Any more questions about time on the barstool?"

It was obvious now that everyone understood what time on the barstool meant. In fact, the regulars paid fast and furious, and Jessie imagined they were emptying out every last bit of money they had.

When the regulars left, a gunman laughed, "Damn, Jane, you really know how to kill a party mood."

"Get that sack of shit outta my face!" Jane shouted at a whore, jerking her shotgun at the dead tax collector.

Sickened by it all, Jessie got up to go outside, wait for Ki, and get some fresh air.

Outside, she found Barabbas. The bounty hunter was slowly riding toward her through the mist with a large buckboard in tow. Grim, she stood there, waiting for him.

★

Chapter 8

Jessie stepped down into the street.

"You ever notice something about this mist?" Barabbas asked, reining in the buckboard, which was drawn by two black geldings.

"What's that?"

"Even when the sun starts to go down, it stays light for awhile. Weird, that's all. I mean, it's as if this place is cursed."

Jessie didn't think of it that way, but she did notice that what Barabbas said had some semblance of truth. It was as if time meant nothing in Apocalypse. The day should have been over; night should have descended. It seemed darker, but the mist was as white as ever.

"What do you think you're doing?" Jessie asked.

"Getting ready."

"You ought to just wear a sign that tells everybody what you are and what you're going to do."

"You know, lady, I've taken just about all the shit off you I can stomach."

Jessie grinned. "Oh?"

"I told you, the games are over. The general's coming, when I don't know, but I'll be ready."

"Your greed is showing. It's sickening." She shook her head. "You know, not that you'd understand, but when you live for money, when you live and work just to make a dollar, somehow it takes the joy out of living; worse, it cheapens and degrades all life around you."

"Who cares? Surely, you're not foolish enough to believe that the world runs on love."

"You see, despite what Bull is, a cold-blooded killer, he still has a heart there. He sees talent; he can see life. I'm talking about The Painter. What's really sad, is The Painter is pure genius. For whatever reason, he's stuck here, at the end of the line. He'll probably die very soon. All he has now is his bottle, and hopefully some memories of better days. The world will be a much sorrier place without him. All that talent, wasted here in this shithole. Genius, that in a way, is being mocked, and is surely being used for wrong. But at least he's using it. Idle hands are dangerous hands." Jessie added, "See, The Painter has no use for money. Hell, I can see him, sitting in his room, in the dark, alone, a nice buzz on to kill the pain, crying out in pure torment, 'Is there anybody out there?' I understand now. I can feel it inside, myself. Once you know it, it never goes away. See, The Painter, he's like Billy; this is what I always saw in Billy. The Painter, he lives only to feel something. He has to feel something or he dies inside, piece by piece. Unfortunately, people like him, and like Billy, they will never find what they so badly need and want. Not in this world. This, Barabbas, or whatever your name is, is the sorrow of the world, this is the tragedy of all life. For the Painter, for Billy, the untruth of the unjust will always be in the way somehow, and that, I believe, is what kills them, too. Someone I once knew—and loved—a man, a real man I loved with as pure a feeling as I'll ever know— he said, you know what he said, God love him, he said, the song is shit. That's what it is. The song is shit. It means everything, and it means nothing. Remember that, Barabbas."

Barabbas peered at Jessie. "After all that, it sounds to me like you just been staring at Bull's oversized sausage a little too long."

Jessie showed the bounty hunter a mean smile. "What I can tell you?" Jessie stood there, suddenly overwhelmed by a burning sadness. She shut her eyes to fight back the tears. "Oh, God, I only wish— I had the powder for The Painter."

"The powder?"

"Yes. The powder. Can you show me where it hurts—*God, can you show me where it hurts?*"

"If you'll excuse me, I got work to do."

"Not without me, you don't."

Barabbas rolled past Jessie.

"I'll see you in about three hours."

Barabbas didn't answer.

"Do you hear me?"

"I heard you."

Jessie watched the bounty hunter vanish into the mist. Alone and afraid, she let a single tear break from her eye, and roll down her cheek. She wondered about Ki. She had hurt him. She was sorry. Very sorry. When he returned, she would tell him how very sorry she was.

"When you were a child, they all went before you, everyone, all of them ghosts that you should have known in the flesh, that you should have loved and who should have loved you. You were alone, and you were afraid, and in your aloneness and your fear you saw the future. What you saw was as a wisp of smoke, fleeing before your eyes. You were a child, your mind at the time could not understand what it was your heart knew."

Thus a potential journey into the future began for Ki.

"What you knew was that the future would be full of pain and sorrow, that you were aware of this in your heart—also you were aware in your heart that all life comes from where it all begins, from the unseen, and that you go finally to where it all ends. When you are aware of this, there is a hunger for truth, for knowledge, for answers, but there is also terrible loneliness, and a yearning, a fire in the belly that will never be quenched, no matter what the world offers you. But, worst of all, you knew you would never have peace in this world if you could not have it as a child. Let me tell you this, this is what I see and this is what I see in you in your struggle—that you are aware that it all comes from the same beginning with no end, and it all goes to eternity. You are deeply aware and troubled, by this, the mystery of life, by the mystery of death, but inside, all of us know that in death the mystery is answered. Still, for some of us it hurts deeper, it clings closer to the surface because we spend our lives searching and wanting to know why. Ki, close your eyes. Relax."

So Ki remained, sitting there at her table, having just finished a second cup of the magic broth that gave him energy and killed his hunger. He stared at Cassandra, thinking she was the most beautiful woman he had ever seen. Never had he heard a voice like hers, so gentle, so soothing. And what she had just told him about himself was true, even though it hurt deep, filled him with sorrow. She knew his soul, this blind woman with the magic broth and the face and the body without age. He was mesmerized. Finally, he shut his eyes. She stood. She moved behind Ki, and he felt her gently massaging his shoulders, then his neck. At first, he thought he might become aroused, but her touch warmed him, relaxed him. Indeed, it felt as if electricity was being poured into him through her fingers. It was good to be touched like this, he thought, with no hint of desire for the flesh, other than touching to comfort the soul.

"Think of nothing," she said. "Free your mind of all troubled thoughts, let your heart be free of all disturbing feelings. Let me take control of your soul, your mind, your heart. I will show you what you need to see."

Ki felt a warm glow spread through him. He relaxed, felt like he was boneless, as the glow intensified and he felt himself tumbling, slowly, deeper and deeper into some hidden dark part of his soul, but it was a part of him that was suddenly being filled with light.

"Yes, Ki, I know, you see them, these ghosts."

He did, but were they ghosts, or were they real people? Or were they something else, and, if so, then what? And how did she know what he was seeing? In his mind, he saw them so clearly, it was as if he was right there. They came through a white haze, floating past him, he couldn't quite see their faces, for they appeared to be moving at a great distance. But he knew, somehow he knew who they were, and he wanted to cry out their names, but his voice wouldn't work. They were his parents and all of his ancestors, drifting toward him, then melting away into the distance. One by one, staring him in the eye from that great distance, having never seen him, but yet knowing exactly who he was, whispering his name as they faded away in the shimmering white haze. A terrible sorrow boiled up in Ki. This was awful, this gut-wrenching loneliness he suddenly felt. She was right. There would never be peace for him in the world.

"Do not be sad, Ki. Do not be afraid. You are not alone. They wait for you, they know you, they know your every thought and feeling, they know the good and the bad in you, they know your sorrow and your joy. The day will come, you will see them, you will be happy and the euphoria you will shortly feel through my fingers will be eternal."

It seemed as if her voice, her touch was right inside of him. Ki was filled with her electric touch, filled with that euphoria she spoke of, a feeling so good, he had never even imagined something like this was possible. Moments later, it felt as if he could float, that he was no longer inside his body, knowing then from that moment on he would always believe his flesh was nothing but a prison, a trap.

"Be still, Ki. Do not think about what is happening, accept it."

The mist suddenly exploded in flames. He jumped, startled.

"Keep your eyes shut, Ki. Do not be alarmed."

The fire raged, then it slowly faded. As the flames vanished, he saw Jessie. She floated toward him, a vision of pure white. Her voice drifted toward him. He strained to hear her voice. She said, "Ki, I am sorry I have hurt you. Forgive me. I love you, I will never leave you. I will never hurt you again. Believe me, please. I am so very sorry."

Then she vanished. He saw what appeared to be three horses, the riders with their backs turned to him. Smoke boiled in black sheets behind them, as they slowly rode off into the distance. There were mountains and snow and sunshine, but the light was so bright, he was partly blinded and could not clearly see their faces. He knew who they were, but he had to know for certain.

"Who are they?"

"You already know, Ki."

He felt her fingers slip away from his neck. Slowly, that feeling of electricity, of peace and ecstasy left him, like water through a sieve.

"You showed me the future," Ki breathed.

For a long moment, she said nothing, then she said, "There is another reason you came back to me. You need love. So do I."

He felt her lips on his neck. Ki moaned. Her lips, like her fingers, filled him once again with that feeling of power and peace, his heart feeling as if it was slowly melting, the glow and the warmth spreading through him again. He felt her lips on his mouth, gentle but fiery, soft but hungry.

She pulled back and he stared into her white eyes.

"I have not known a man since my husband," she told him. "Indeed, my husband was the only man I ever knew, and ever loved. I believe I could love you—more than anyone. We need to love each other. If only just this once."

She stood and took off her clothes. Her body was an incredible sight to Ki. She was so beautiful, her skin so smooth and firm, so white and pure, he felt he could stare at her forever. She had the body and the skin of a teenage girl, soft and creamy and unblemished, yet he knew she had to be well up in years. It fascinated and spooked Ki a little that she seemed ageless. And he noticed for the first time the smell of her skin, as she asked him to stand then slowly began undressing him. She smelled of honey and perfume, of the freshest sweetest flowers ever to grow. As he sat and she knelt before him, Ki began to wonder if this was really happening, if she was even real, alive. He wondered if she was some kind of hallucination or a dream. Was she an angel?

Hypnotized by her beauty, he watched as she took his hardening member in her hand. He groaned, his eyes closing, feeling powerless, completely in her control as she gently stroked him with her hands, then settled her mouth on his swollen head. He wanted it to last forever, as he shivered, her mouth, a tight watery suckling thing, hungrily taking his full length. As she sucked, she made little moaning and slurping noises that inflamed him with a maddening need to go into her.

Finally, she stood, spread her legs, and sat down on him, slowly, using her hand, guiding him into her. She was sopping wet, tight, fiery. He spread her ass with his hands. She locked her mouth on Ki's mouth, grinding herself into him, her musk and the scent of her flesh like a narcotic that made him float, then sink into the feeling of ecstasy, as he seized that feeling, wanting more and more of her. He felt himself on the verge of erupting, as her thrusting, her sliding up and down him became more furious, her breath flaming into his lungs, her cries ringing in his ears. He bent his head, took her breast in his mouth, her nipple swollen and huge. She breathed into his ear that she was coming. Right then, Ki felt free and untroubled, accepted and loved.

Ki felt her shudder in his arms as she screamed in orgasm. His hands cupped around the silky smoothness of her buttocks, he picked her up, still deep in her. She writhed and cried as he laid her down on the floor, sliding out of her, then mounting her, going in slowly, deeply. He pushed her legs back, making it last, making her feel him, deep and wide and hard, wanting her sore and aching, wanting her to still feel him even when he was long gone.

He cried out her name, kissed her as he came.

He stayed hard, even after the last spurt. There was something about this woman, her beauty, her power, the beauty of her heart, the sweet melody of her voice, the strength of her words, the wisdom inside her that made him want her again and again.

He stayed inside her. He went in and out of her slowly, tormenting her, before she shook and cried as another orgasm wracked her body.

Finally, he felt himself shrivel up and slip out of her.

Her face seemed to glow with pleasure beneath him. Gently, tenderly, Ki kissed her.

She touched Ki's face. "You must go now, Ki. She waits for you."

Ki felt sad at the thought of having to leave Cassandra.

It felt like it took a great effort, but he dressed. Naked still, Cassandra came to Ki. They embraced. When he looked at her, he saw she was grim.

"Listen, Ki, I have shown you what is ahead. However, be warned. There is a chance it will not end the way you have seen it, the way you want it to. There are other things I did not show you.

Listen to me, and do not ask questions. Please. They will come soon. There will be many of them, then there will be four others to follow. They will be like wild animals and they will devour many before they meet a terrible end. There will be much suffering and much bloodshed. You must stay strong and not concern yourself to the point of endangering your own life over her. Trust your heart."

He waited for her to say more, but. she stayed silent.

"Go now. Perhaps someday, Ki, you will return here. I will pray for you and hope the best. Hope is all that is left for the good heart."

He started to say something to her, but she put a finger on his lips.

Silently, Ki left her home.

He had hoped to leave her feeling alive and good. But when he was outside in the darkness, he found himself once again becoming afraid and angry, and he felt that terrible, gut-wrenching aloneness.

★

Chapter 9

When they were asleep in Hell and a silence as heavy as death fell over Apocalypse, Jessie and Barabbas began to search the town for Billy Johnson.

They had already searched several buildings and found them empty. They had gone through several dozen sulfur matches to light their way. In the large stable they discovered several bullet-riddled corpses, frozen stiff. None of them was Billy.

Bullwhip around her shoulder, her hand never far from her revolver, Jessie led Barabbas into the lobby of the town hotel. No one was in there, but there was kerosene light shining from the upstairs hallway.

Ki had not returned, and Jessie was becoming concerned, wondering if he might be gone for good or if something had happened to him. She wished he would come back to her. Her heart was heavy with sorrow and dread.

They moved upstairs, into the soft glow of light from a lantern hung from the ceiling.

Suddenly, the sound of a door creaking from below broke the silence. Jessie looked at Barabbas. Had they been spotted searching the buildings? Followed?

Jessie opened a door and found the room empty. She nodded for Barabbas to follow her inside. She closed the door only far enough so that there was still a crack. She waited, listening to the sound of spurs jingling. She sensed danger.

There were two of them. Both had revolvers in their hands. As they walked past the door, she slipped the whip off her shoulder. Then she stepped out into the hallway.

The whip scorched the air and sent one, then two revolvers flying down the hall. Startled, they began to turn. Barabbas flattened one of them with a bone-crunching right to the jaw, then he stepped on the guy's throat, crushing his windpipe. Before the other one could get a good look at her face, Jessie wrapped the bullwhip around his throat and wrenched. He was small, maybe five and a half feet tall, and thin, but he fought like a tiger. He tried to claw Jessie's eyes. Adrenaline surged through her and with rage and fear-powered strength, she lifted him off his feet. The guy croaked and clawed at air, trying to blind Jessie, as Jessie dragged him down the hall, toward the steps. His legs flailing, Jessie lifted him off his feet, then hurled him down on a large wooden knob attached to the railing. The guy came down hard on his balls, and there was an awful crunching sound, but his scream was choked off by the whip cutting deep into his throat.

"Stop struggling," Jessie hissed into his bulging eyes, "or I'll rip your head off!"

But the man kept clawing, somehow ripping open her blouse. Her breasts fell out, and hardened nipples poked into the back of his neck.

"Where's the boy, Billy Johnson?" Jessie snarled quietly into his ear, releasing some of the pressure.

"You're—dead, bitch! Knew—you came here—for the—kid—"

Somehow, the guy grabbed a knife from his pants leg. Fear exploding through her, Jessie squeezed harder and harder on the whip, dodging the razor-sharp edge of the blade as it swept past her face. The guy gagged, drool spilling from his mouth as Jessie strangled the life out of him.

She released the whip, let the dead weight drop at her feet, her bared breasts heaving from exertion. She covered herself.

Barabbas helped her get the bodies of their attackers hidden in the room. But two more armed shadows were waiting for them when they stepped out into the hall.

One of the shadows grinned, but Jessie didn't recognize either man.

"The kid ain't for sale, bitch. Say good night, you and your boyfriend."

"Bull will love this, won't he, Tony? Killin' these two—"

The guy never finished his statement. Suddenly, he was twitching, his gun falling from his hand, as he grabbed at something in the back of his neck. As he turned, Jessie glimpsed the throwing star reflecting kerosene light, sticking in the back of his neck. Tony was overwhelmed by the flying shadow of Ki. Ki locked his arms around the guy's throat and snapped his neck like a twig. To silence the other gunman's croaking, Ki crushed his throat with a knife-edged hand. As soon as the guy crumpled, Ki and Jessie dragged the men into the room.

Once again, Jessie heard the downstairs door open. Wild-eyed, she looked at Ki. Barabbas stepped into the room, then quietly closed the door, his gun drawn. Iron in hand, Jessie and Ki moved to the door, stood beside Barabbas, waiting, listening. Whoever was out there was big, and in a hurry, as he bounded up the steps. The sound of boots pounded past their door, moving down the hall. Carefully, Jessie opened the door a crack. She saw Bull, fully dressed, barging through a door at the end of the hall, slamming it shut.

Jessie heaved a breath. "Well, it looks like our little search just ended."

"But we know the kid's here in town at least," Barabbas said.

For a long moment, Jessie stared at Ki. He looked sad. Jessie's heart ached. Her mouth opened, but the words she wanted to say so badly wouldn't come out.

"Think it best we call it a night, come up with a new strategy," Ki said.

Jessie nodded. Then she heard a noise, like a man crying. Curious, she ventured out into the hall and moved to the door that Bull had gone through. She stood there, listening to the muffled sobs beyond the door. Jessie put her hand on the knob, then felt Ki's hand on her shoulder.

She looked at Ki, who shook his head. Gun in hand, she whispered, "It's okay."

Her heart pounding, anxious to know what was happening beyond the door, she turned the knob, praying it didn't creak. This was perhaps a dangerous and stupid move, she thought, but she was ready for anything.

What she wasn't prepared for was the sight of Bull, kneeling beside the bed of The Painter, tears rolling down the big man's cheeks.

Jessie couldn't believe her eyes at first. It was like a dream. Soft kerosene light flickered over the face of Bull, the whores Donna and Rachel, and The Painter, who was stretched out, naked in bed. The Painter was staring up at the ceiling. For a second, Jessie thought the old man was dead. Then an awful croaking sound emerged from The Painter's lips.

Bull clasped his hands together, as if in prayer, shut his eyes, and bowed his head. Donna and Rachel hung back, staring at Bull. Both of the whores looked terribly afraid. The Painter kept croaking, trying to say something, but no words came out.

Jessie quietly closed the door. She'd seen enough.

She feared tomorrow was not going to be a good day in Hell.

The Painter died early in the morning, just after sunup.

Jessie heard the dreaded news as she was eating a steak, Ki beside her, picking at a plate of potatoes, sullen and worried.

Donna and Rachel, looking terrified, stumbled into the saloon. Their expressions, and their silence said it all. Donna asked, in a quavering voice, for someone to go get Bull.

Jessie stopped eating. A heavy silence descended over the few whores and the gunmen who were up and drinking and gambling at that early hour.

A whore hesitated before knocking on Bull's door.

"What?"

Not good, Jessie thought, hearing Bull's booming voice, knowing Bull was in a very foul mood.

"Bull—uh, Donna and Rachel—they need to see you—"

The door opened suddenly. Bull shoved the whore aside. He was dressed only in black Levi's, a nearly empty bottle in his hand. He staggered toward Donna and Rachel. The whores stepped back. Bull was good and drunk already, looking like he'd been up all night long.

The awful silence that hung between the whores and Bull dragged out.

Jessie watched, afraid of what was going to happen.

Bull looked at the whores for what seemed like an eternity.

"Bull—I—"

"What? What!" Bull roared, making them flinch and cringe before him. "No. No."

Over and over, Bull said no, as the whores cried how sorry they were.

"He's—no—"

"He's dead, Bull," Donna said.

Bull crumpled to his knees and bellowed. The walls and the floor seemed to tremble with Bull's cry of anguish and rage. Then Bull became strangely silent and still. Donna and Rachel—indeed, everyone—just looked at each other, waiting in terror. Suddenly, Bull began sobbing. The whores sidled away from Bull.

Had Jessie not seen this with her own eyes, a grown man, a tough guy, a cold-blooded killer, weeping his eyes out over the death of another man, a strange and tormented and disturbed man but one who had a very rare gift, she would not have believed it. She was shocked by the sight of his grief, then she felt sorry for Bull.

An idea formed in her mind—that new strategy Ki had mentioned.

They buried The Painter just outside of town.

Jessie, Ki, and Barabbas watched from a distance. Bull had raged for everyone to get dressed, get their sorry asses outside, and now. He had ordered four volunteers to set fire to the ground to thaw it out. Dressed in a long sheepskin coat, Bull waited while his volunteers hacked at the ground with picks and shovels. It was so cold, the tears had frozen on Bull's face.

Bull performed the ceremony. Gently he placed the Painter's body in a wooden box and put the box in the ground. He placed the Painter's easel, brushes, and smock on top of the coffin along with a fresh bottle of whiskey. Then he told the men to cover him up. When The Painter was buried, Bull bellowed for everyone to get the hell away from him, that all of them were unworthy to even be there beside him in his time of grief, that their very presence was a desecration to the memory of such a great and noble man. Everyone looked all too relieved to leave Bull alone.

Jessie watched as Bull knelt and wept and mouthed words she could not make out.

Finally, Bull stood and strode toward the saloon. Jessie waited, then followed him inside. Bull roared that he wanted to be left alone and disappeared into his room.

Jessie sat at her table. Everyone looked afraid and uncomfortable. In sullen and fearful silence, gunmen drank and played cards.

Jessie let a full two hours pass. She felt the eyes of Barabbas and Ki on her. She looked at both men.

"So, what's the plan?" Barabbas asked, firing up a smoke. "You look like you got something in mind."

Jessie plucked up a bottle. She grinned at Barabbas. She told him, "I'd appreciate some privacy, a little time for me to, uh, I guess, grab the bull by the horns."

Ki looked at Jessie with fear in his eyes. "Jessie, you're not going to his room, are you? He's insane!"

"So am I."

Jessie walked toward Bull's door. She looked back at Ki and Barabbas. She caught the look of shame, perhaps even a flicker of jealousy in the eyes of Barabbas. She felt strong and in control even though she was pushing it as she knocked on Bull's door.

"Goddammit, I told you, I want to be left alone!"

"Bull, please, it's me, Jessie."

Silence.

"You? All right. You can come in. No one else!"

His voice sounded soft and tender for just a moment there. Jessie felt some hope as she turned the knob and entered Bull's room.

★

Chapter 10

When she was alone with Bull in his room, Jessie felt her confidence flee. She stood there for many awful moments, intimidated, afraid, as the big Indian stood before her, dressed only in Levi's, a bottle in his hand, his stare penetrating, suspicious. She glanced around the large room to break his piercing gaze. Furs were piled everywhere. Whiskey bottles and women's undergarments were scattered in soiled heaps beside Bull's large bed that was covered with the skins of mountain lions and bears and buffalo hide. Looming over her in the low yellow light flickering from a kerosene lantern, he suddenly looked especially frightening to her.

"You don't come to me as another whore, lusting for what I have between my legs," Bull said, then sucked down the rest of his bottle, grabbed a fresh one, and broke it open. "You are different. I can tell. You are a woman of heart and substance. So. White Woman of Heart and Substance, what is it you want from Bull?"

"I—I just wanted to tell you how terribly sorry I am about The Painter."

He peered at her. "You know something—I believe you. But I sense you want something else. What?"

Jessie stood there, found her gaze wandering over the huge bulge in his pants. "I—I uh, just—that. I'm sorry. I didn't think you would want to be alone. I—would like to comfort you. I come to you—as a friend."

He smiled, a smile of genuine warmth. "You are different, you are special. A woman such as you, especially a white woman, is rare. Please. Sit with me for awhile. Let Bull talk."

She sat beside Bull. He drank, offered her the bottle, and Jessie drank, too.

"You are—so beautiful. I mean that with all my heart, Jessie. Indeed, I will refer to you from here on as the Most Beautiful of White Women. That will be your name. Most Beautiful of White Women."

Jessie was flattered. "Thank you."

"Do not thank me. To me, no matter who the woman, she is still a woman. A woman's heart, no matter how pure at one time, can become deceitful and vile. But that is all right. Men can be the same, but it is different when men become that way. A man must stay strong. Women are weak. They are expected to be weak and at times vile and deceitful. This is their nature. See, I understand

104

something about life. Let Bull tell you something about life. The human heart is a dark thing. Only when we are children are we innocent and in our purest state. But as the child grows, this, sadly, leaves. What dreams of goodness there were, they die, what was pure and innocent, it dies, for what is real is not pretty, what is real is death. You see, it all flees before us toward death. This is why I grieve so much for The Painter. He was a man, but he stayed as a child. Do not misunderstand me on this. The Painter was very sick in his own way, perhaps even more sick than the rest of us. His gift also brought him a special madness, a special sight into this darkness of the human heart." Bull paused, a tear breaking suddenly from the corner of his eye. "Do you know, I never even knew his name? I only knew him as The Painter. I was very selfish with him. Bull, he used The Painter's rare talent for what is sickness. I hope I pay with much suffering for what I did to him, in my selfishness. I see you are—surprised. My grief truly shocks you."

"Yes. It does."

"Because I kill and lay with whores in the open? Because I put garbage in their own filth? Ah!" He threw his hand out, as if dismissing something or someone. "They are garbage out there, that is what and all they are. But—so am I. They— indeed, all of us—we are doomed to die, we deserve to die, we deserve suffering. That is okay. I accept death, and suffering, it makes a man stronger if he suffers like a man to begin with. I only hope— and here I am sure you will be surprised again to hear me talk like this—I only hope that the Great One will accept my unworthy soul, a soul that is perhaps even unworthy of a warrior's death."

Jessie was taken aback for a second.

"Understand, Most Beautiful of White Women: Bull, he sees a rare gift, he knows when someone is special. The Painter, he, his gift, it was—like a bolt of lightning from the Great One. It is at once a blessing and a curse, such a rare talent as he had. He saw and he felt and his heart— I believe his heart only longed to be loved. But, because of the impurity of the world, and, yes, the impurity in his own heart, the darkness in his own soul, it could never be. He knew this. He would never be loved as he should. He knew that love, like life itself, is but a fleeting thing, rushing toward death. He knew that all must end in death, in sorrow and pain and grieving. He knew that none of us are worthy of true and real love. This was his torment. I miss him badly. I will grieve for days. But—I know he is at peace now. Ah, but The Painter should have had the world, everything he wanted. Indeed, I believe the world owed him that. But The Painter did not want the world. That, too, made him special." He paused to drink, a deep swallow that drained half the bottle. "You see, I always wanted to do something, to be something special. I wanted to create something with my hands, but I do not have the talent. I can see it, however. When I see it and it is real, my heart is full of joy. The world, it is such a sad and sorry place. There are too few men like The Painter." He stared at Jessie, her mouth. "You say you come to comfort me. Understand, for now, you must be my whore, my white whore, it is the only way Bull can become aroused. Later—later, I will think of you as my lady. Kiss me. Kiss me gently, you will do as I say, or you will upset me much. And I know you do not want to upset me any more than I already am. You will use your body for me to ease my pain."

It was far too late to change her mind now; Jessie knew she was committed. She had already decided to give herself to this man.

"Stand up. Take off your clothes. Let me feast my eyes on your beauty."

Somehow, with trembling fingers, Jessie stood and undressed. How would she play this? She had come here wanting information about Billy Johnson. But, no, this was not the time to upset Bull any more. Her heart suddenly burning with lust, she felt herself melting inside, her legs weak.

She stood, naked before Bull. He sipped his whiskey, his eyes afire with lust, as he looked her up and down.

"Turn around."

She did. Gently, he smacked her on the ass.

"Maybe you shall stay my woman, my only woman. Would you like that?"

"I—don't know—"

"Okay. Not yet. I understand."

Jessie took the huge meat in her hands, stared at it for many moments, the moisture between her legs flowing like lava. Bull's cock grew and hardened before her eyes. She moaned as she kissed the swollen head, big as a doorknob. She heard Bull chuckle. She was his whore for the moment, but for some reason, she accepted that, indeed, she wanted that. She looked up, smiled at Bull as she stroked his cock with both hands, before she began running her wet mouth up and down the length of his pole.

Jessie groaned, pulled her mouth off him, then began pumping him in a frenzy, crying, "I can't stand it. Put it in me."

"Not yet. Only when Bull is ready to pleasure you."

Thus Bull made her suck some more, then finally pulled her to her feet. He made her stand there as he prodded her fiery wetness with his fingers, making her writhe and squirm and beg to be filled. She collapsed, dizzy from want, into his big muscular arms, kissing him hard on the mouth. As if she weighed no more than a feather, he picked her up. Jessie opened her legs as far as they would go, afraid of what was next. Bull chuckled as Jessie, letting out a piercing scream, felt that monster thing begin to penetrate her. Slowly, crying and throwing her head around, straddled against him, she took it in. She thought she was going to be split in half. Jessie cried his name, over and over, her eyes shut, her teeth gritted. She mashed her breasts against the corded muscles of his chest, falling into a rhythm, sliding up and down, Bull kneading her ass. She threw her arms around his neck, then bit his shoulder as orgasm exploded through her. She thrashed, and Bull pumped harder. He laid her down, slid out of her. He made her lie on her side, lifted one of her legs, and pierced her sopping wetness from behind, rubbing her hardened swollen nipples. Feeling powerless, Jessie just let him take her, slow, then fast, then slow again, as he pulled her leg up as high as it would go. As she felt herself coming again, she thought she would faint.

Exhausted, Jessie collapsed in the furs, purring like a kitten. Bull rolled a smoke and drank some whiskey, while Jessie fell asleep. When she woke, feeling like her insides had been ripped out, she found herself in Bull's arms, one leg draped over his stomach.

"What—how long was I asleep?"

Bull smoked, drank, smiled down at her. "Not long. Two hours maybe."

Jessie decided now was the time to do it. She steeled herself, afraid of Bull's reaction.

"Bull. I—I have something to tell you. I—I was not completely honest about why I'm here. I mean, right now, with you."

"Ah. You mean you have deceived me?"

"I—well, in a way. But I wanted to be here with you."

"I see. Well, that is all right. I know the story of your Eve, the mother of all women, how she deceived the first man. So, you see, all women, even one as you, Most Beautiful of White Women, are deceitful creatures. It is simply the nature of a woman to lie."

"Well, thanks."

"You are welcome," Bull grinned to Jessie's sarcasm. "So, tell me, what is this deceit?"

"It is about someone—I came here to find—"

Bull grunted, a strange glint in his eyes. "A boy perhaps? Young, with blond hair, skinny. Writes poetry. Ahhhh, yes. The one I now know as Billy Johnson?"

Jessie sat up.

"Relax. He is safe. Indeed, he shall remain safe as long as Bull protects him."

"Bull, please—I need to talk to him. I mean him no harm."

"I know, Jessica Starbuck. I know all about you. You were, how shall I put it, like the boy's mother for some time. Until you cast him off to the wilderness."

Jessie was surprised, afraid. "Bull, I don't know what he told you, but it wasn't like that."

"Once again, for some reason, I believe you."

"Where is he? Please. His life is in danger."

Bull chuckled. "You should never underestimate Bull."

"Bull, please, where is he?"

"Where? Why, he is right here. In this room."

★

Chapter 11

"Do not be so quick to think Bull will favor you like this! Be still, white woman! Listen to me!"

Jessie dressed, pushing her luck, as Bull snarled at her again to be still and listen to him.

"Damn you!" Bull rasped, as Jessie stood before him, fully dressed and armed. "The boy, he is my property!"

"Property! Like—like—"

"No, not like that. That is an abomination, a man does not lie with a man! By property, I mean he is my Painter, too, but as a poet. Should I not know his name, I would call him The Poet. He is special, he has a gift like that of The Painter. He is under Bull's protection! I see this garbage that hangs out in the saloon, waiting, sharpening their blades, hoping to make much money off his blood. It shall not be."

"If you know who I am, then you know I mean him no harm."

"Oh? Perhaps you come to take him away from Bull. This would also be like death. I will not permit it."

"Let him make up his own mind about that. He is in trouble. The law wants him for murder."

"He murdered no one, he only removed another whore from the world. Let me tell you his story."

The silence dragged out. Jessie waited. Then she told Bull, "Go on, I'm listening."

"It happened in a small town, many many hundreds of miles back East. There was a young whore who had run away from her father, a rich man back East. This man, he sent guns to find her, these white men with guns to kill any man who had harmed his daughter. Little did the father know that this whore, this creature the father foolishly cherished so much, was as vile and deceitful as any white woman. That, had she lived, she would have only brought much grief and sorrow into the lives of many men. Now, my young William, he drinks much, to kill the pain of all that is, will not be, and was not. This I understand like no one else, this aching sorrow of the soul, this swollen ball of fire that is always in the belly. Now. Young William, he wanted this whore, but she wanted money from him. This creature, I see it all in my mind, she has no heart, thus, how can she see heart? She only wants money. Indeed, when I see this white creature of vileness in my mind, it makes me sick. Now. Bull does not have the problem many men do, what we shall call 'whiskey dick.' Now, listen, this is the story of the whiskey dick. I shall later put in my own interpretation of this.

"Billy, he gets into bed with this white creature of deceit and vileness. He cannot perform. She laughs at him, shames him. Finally, he becomes aroused, not good, but good enough to empty himself into this despicable creature."

"He told you all this?"

"Woman, he told me everything, I am the father he never had. Listen to me! I know his heart, I know his soul, like The Painter, his talent—Have I not mentioned it before I do now. He, young William, is a poet—it, his poetry, his beautiful words, they bring light into this terrible place of darkness. Now. Young William, he trusts me, this is all you really need to know. Now. May I finish the story of the whiskey dick?"

"Are you asking or telling me?"

"I am telling you to be silent, white woman! Now. This creature, this whore, she is unsatisfied, she still shames him, she has the heart of a devil, she is also interested only in the flesh, in being satisfied by big and hard meat in her, thus, once again, here I am, filled with sickness. Billy, he only dumped himself in this whore to keep some respect as a man. He drinks more, he has money. The creature, she steals his money, then she holds a knife to his throat, rousing him from sleep. The creature, she says he shamed her. Can you believe that? She wants more money. She says she knows he has more. He will get it or the creature will cut his throat. Indeed, my young William, he tells me, a part of him feels sorry for this worthless creature of white skin, she is so pitiful and despicable. Now. William, he is scared and shamed and sorry for this creature, because he has heart, and this creature is without shame. The white female creature, she tries to stab him. He reacts, he hits her, she falls on, of all things, his whiskey bottle. The bottle, it breaks, a piece of glass pierces her neck and kills her. Now. I say to you, 'Is this not justice? Is this not the hand of the Great One at work?' Were it I, I would have been much upset because she broke my only bottle of whiskey, not because she is dead. But William, afraid, he runs. Thus, he ends up here, in Hell, after many many months of being hunted by this father's gunmen. And that, Most Beautiful of White Women, that is the sad story of the whiskey dick."

For many moments, Jessie was silent. She looked at Bull, who seemed angry with her.

"You look at me funny. Do not upset me, white woman, lest I lose all respect for you. You do not want that."

"No, I don't. And I'm not upset with you."

"Can you not see? Can you not understand? How a creature like that can be so without honor, so without respect and shame, that she can drive a man, a good man, to do terrible things? How a creature like that, living only for money and meat, can rip the heart and the soul out of a good man?"

"Yes. Yes, Bull, believe me, I see it."

"I believe you do. I believe you do." Bull smoked

in silence for several moments. "The heart of a woman, it can be a blessing, it can be a curse. This is what Bull sees. A good woman is a rare find, it happens once, maybe twice in a man's life if he is lucky. Thus, a man, once he has this rare diamond, she should be worshipped and cherished. Indeed, he should be prepared to die for her. My heart, it can be soft for such a woman. Sadly, I have never had this diamond. I see what most women are, that they offer what they have between their legs in exchange for life, that they can use what they stupidly think is like gold to trap a man, to steal his money, his heart, his soul. Is not the woman who is a whore like the hungry wolf in hunt of good meat?"

"Bull, forgive me for saying this, but I'd have to say that you have a very negative opinion of women."

"Am I wrong?"

"Uh—to some extent, but, no, I think you are right. I mean, well, I see the kind of women you have out there."

"Whores! Of course! But in the hearts of most women, there is the whore!"

Jessie stared at Bull for several seconds. How could she argue with all that, especially when there was some degree of truth to what Bull said? She swallowed hard, frightened of, but also fond of this man, finding herself liking him very much despite his twisted and narrow view of women. In some way, she understood how he could feel the way he did.

"You will be my good woman, my diamond?"

What could she say to that? Jessie wondered. A part of her wanted to say yes, but another part pulled back.

"We'll see," she said.

Bull's gaze narrowed, and he grunted, "All right. I respect you. So. We'll see."

Jessie sucked in a deep breath, paused, then said, "Bull? I ask you one more time. Please. Let me see Billy."

Bull stood and slipped on his black Levi's. He leveled a piercing stare at Jessie for a long moment, then grunted for her to follow him.

Bull moved to the far corner of the room. There, he pulled back a door. Behind the door, Jessie saw him.

Billy Johnson had not changed much since she'd last seen him. He sat there on the edge of his bed, alone, a bottle of whiskey in his hand, looking every bit as lost and lonely and pathetic as any of the happy hour regulars. Beside him was a notepad and pen. Jessie stared at Billy, his soft face, his thin blond hair, his skinny, almost spindly frame. Billy looked uncertain, then annoyed. He looked so very young to Jessie, the new Jessie, the old and wise Pandora, but she could tell his eyes had seen sorrow and death, that his eyes were the eyes of an old man.

"Billy?"

For many moments, Billy Johnson said nothing, just stared at Jessie, as if seeing a stranger. Then he nodded, a wan smile on his lips.

"Jessie. I wasn't sure if I wanted to see you or not," Billy said. "I'm still not sure. And if you came here to take me away, I'm not going."

Jessie heaved a breath, then moved into the small, cluttered room.

"Remember what I said to you, white woman," Bull growled. "I leave you two alone. Do not upset my young William."

Ki walked out of Hell to get some fresh air and to be alone. He stood there in the middle of the street, shaking his head, grunting, wondering where it was all going.

Then he heard them.

Like ghosts, they appeared in the mist, riding slowly into town from the east. As they parted the white mist and headed his way, Ki saw the Confederate flag, saw the black flag with a white skull and crossbones. Horses whickered, sabers rattled, and leather creaked.

Perhaps three dozen silent, grim-faced riders emerged from the mist, all of them heavily armed. Their eyes burned with anger and contempt for everything and everyone in the path of their march.

Ki felt something icy shiver down his back. He felt as if he had seen these men before.

Indeed, he had.

Ki sucked in a deep breath as they closed on him, looking at him with contempt and raw hatred in their eyes.

It came to him. In his mind, he heard Cassandra's warning. *"They will come soon. There will be many of them—they will be like wild animals and they will devour many."*

They stopped in front of the saloon named Hell, still staring down Ki, who didn't move. Some of them spat, some grunted, but all of them dismounted, almost at the same instant, their hands draped over gun butts or the hilts of sabers.

When they disappeared inside Hell, Ki, worried about Jessie, followed them inside.

"Jessie, please understand, I have found a home here. Bull cares about me very much."

Jessie sighed, sat beside Billy, staring deeply into his old eyes. "Billy, I never meant to hurt you."

"But you did."

"I am not your enemy."

"You threw me out of your home. And after all I'd been through."

"You stole from me. Not just once, but many times. You were uncontrollable. You can't see yourself, how you are when you drink. You become ugly and mean and belligerent."

Billy looked away from Jessie, his eyes sad. He took a sip of whiskey. "I didn't mean to kill that girl. You should've heard what she said to me. I have never been talked to like that in all my life—not even by my own mother, who hated me."

"I don't know that she hated you, Billy."

"You weren't there, you never saw the way she beat me. The worst thing, it was how she—died. That was the final act of bitterness and ugliness on her part."

"Oh, God."

Jessie put her arms around Billy, cradled his face to her bosom. She felt him shudder, then heard his quiet sobs.

"It's okay, Billy. It's all right. Bull told me what happened. I know you didn't mean to kill her, I know she hurt you."

He laughed a strange laugh. "You know, Jessie, you holding me like this—I used to dream about you—you know—what—what it might be like. Can I tell you something?"

"Yes. Please do."

"I wrote a poem about you. I showed Bull. He—you know what he said? He said it was the most beautiful thing he'd ever read. And he reads all the time, he reads everything, he especially loves poetry. He—you know what he did? He cried when he read my poem about you. Well, actually, it was part of several poems I had put together. It's called 'The World's on Fire.' He said I should sell it, that I could be famous. I've never seen someone like him—someone who can care so much. I don't want to leave this place."

Jessie pulled back, touched Billy's face, wiped the tears off with her fingers. "Listen to me, Billy. This girl you—killed accidentally. Her father is rich and powerful, he is sending men, bad men after you, men who will kill you as easily as they would shoot a rattlesnake. There is a bounty on your head. Even now, there are men in the room outside who would kill you for the money."

"Bull's protecting me."

"But for how long? And what are you going to do? Just sit in this room forever?"

"It's safe here. Bull brings me everything. I eat good, I have all the whiskey I want, all the smokes, he brings me a woman sometimes and tells her to please me or else—"

Jessie snorted at this foolishness. "You're so young."

"Yeah, you think of me as just a kid, just a boy."

"No—"

"Yes, you do."

"I think of you—maybe as the son I never had."

Billy stared at Jessie through his wet eyes, shocked.

"I do."

"Jessie—I have a confession to make to you. You know, I always—I always wanted you to be—you know, the first woman I was ever with."

Jessie smiled.

"It's true. In fact—I'm not ashamed of this— but—at nights, when I was alone—I would think of you all the time—and—fool with myself—think-ing about your body, your beautiful face—touch-ing your breasts—kissing your mouth—being—in you—like a man—"

Jessie was becoming uncomfortable. She put her finger on his lips. "Say no more."

"I upset you?"

"No. It's just that it can never be."

"And, you see, that is why I am so tormented—"

"No, it isn't, Billy. You can't think of me that way. I'm too old for you."

He frowned, looking like a spoiled child to Jessie. "I figured you'd say something like that."

"Billy, I care about you, but not like that. You are very special to me. Don't ruin what I feel for you. Please."

Still frowning, Billy looked away from Jessie. "Leave me alone. I just want to get drunk. Just leave. Maybe you shouldn't of come here, anyway."

Suddenly, Jessie heard a commotion beyond the walls of Billy's room. It sounded like cursing and yelling and flesh striking flesh. Alarmed, drawing her weapon, Jessie stood.

"What is it?" Billy cried.

Jessie moved into Bull's room. Bull was nowhere to be found. She saw Billy following her, told him to be quiet.

Jessie opened the door just a crack. She froze.

The saloon was filled with thirty or forty men, many of them dressed in the uniform of the Confederacy. One of them, a tall, broad man in a black leather coat that reached to his knees, announced, "Everyone relax and no one gets hurt. General Misery has arrived in Hell to save the day, to, uh, bring peace and happiness and love for all. Okay, people, bottom line here, I'm in charge now. Anyone have a problem with that?"

Jessie closed the door, her heart pounding with fear. She looked at Billy and asked, "Is there another way out of here?"

Billy jerked a nod. "Yes. What's wrong? Who are those men?"

"Demons."

★

Chapter 12

"All right, asshole, just step back, and keep your hands where we can see them."

Ki looked at the guy, a one-armed, toothless guy in a white beard with a saber drawn. With a slit-eyed gaze, Ki looked around the saloon. This was not going to be pretty.

Indeed, it got ugly right away.

As he moved to take a chair at his table, General Misery and his renegade troops got to work. Bull sat on his divan, watching with an impassive face, though Ki saw the rage simmering in his gaze. The patrons of Hell were outnumbered, outgunned, and maybe for the first and last time, they were intimidated by an evil greater than their own.

The soldiers opened up fresh bottles of whiskey, grabbed whores, kissing them, then slapping them around. When she protested about them taking her whiskey, Jane was belted to the floor, her clothes sheared off by flashing sabers. She screamed, was jerked to her feet, trickles of blood rolling down the front of her. Naked, she was shoved to the floor in front of the bar, told to lie there and wait for the fun to begin.

"Who's in charge here?" General Misery barked. "Or, rather, who *was* in charge here?"

Several of the patrons looked toward Bull.

"Him?" General Misery snarled. "Damn Injun! You white people answer to that? You're a disgrace to your own blood! Oh, Jesus, what's the world coming to, anyway?" General Misery shook his head, disgusted. "So. What's your name, Injun?" He walked up to Bull, drew his saber. The general glanced down at the meat outlined against Bull's pants. "God damn, you are a big buck. The head cock here, right? All these pretty white sluts going down on that, huh? Jesus. God damn, what a sorry lot you people are! All right, talk, asshole!" The general rested the edge of his blade on Bull's manhood. "You got a name?"

Bull didn't flinch. "I am called Bull," he said without looking at General Misery.

The general chuckled. "Well, from now on, you'll be called Bullshit. And any bullshit out of you, *Bullshit*, you'll lose that piece of meat. Now. You got any problem with me and the boys taking what we want?"

Silence.

Ki waited, watched.

Bull said, "You will take what you want whether I like it or not."

General Misery erupted in laughter. "God damn, Injun, I may come to like you yet. How 'bout you whores?" He looked at the whores, all of them cringing, some of them, the naked ones, being fondled by the soldiers. "Any problems with givin' me and the boys here a taste? And for free, I'm talking about. I mean, we been in the saddle, without a bitch, for a long time. I mean, it's been a long, hard, cold winter for us. We need pussy heat, we need love."

"Eat shit and die, asshole!" Rachel snarled.

"Oh, a fighter." The general walked right up to Rachel, smiling. He wrenched a handful of her hair. Rachel yelped as he pulled her head back. "Looks like I need to make an example, show everyone here I mean business. But, thank you, anyway, for that little outburst, you slut."

And General Misery drew the blade across the soft white pulsing skin of Rachel's throat. A whore gasped as Rachel's blood spurted over her face. The general held her head back, letting the river of blood run for a moment, then dumped her on the floor, facedown in her blood.

"How 'bout you men here?" the general growled. Then he jerked a nod at a short, fat soldier. "Gimbles! I don't like the way I'm being looked at here!"

With a twisted grin, Gimbles walked up to a male patron, drew his revolver, jammed the muzzle in the guy's ear, and pulled the trigger. Blood and brains flew across the bar.

Ki tensed as several pairs of eyes looked his way.

But Tom, the ex-judge, trying to make himself small, finished his beer, sidled away from the bar, diverting everyone's attention from Ki.

Tom almost reached the door, but General Misery bellowed, "Hey!"

Ki would have sworn that Tom, though freezing in his tracks, jumped about six inches off the floor. Slowly, Tom turned.

"Y-yes."

"It's 'Yes sir,' mister!" General Misery barked at Tom.

"Y-yes—sir."

"Why you leaving, mister?"

"I—don't know—"

"I didn't excuse you, you're not dismissed."

"I—I—I—"

General Misery laughed, took several steps toward Tom. "You what?"

"I—I don't know—"

"You don't know much, do you, mister. What you should do, right now, is ask me, 'General, sir, am I dismissed?' "

Tom swallowed hard, his legs shaking as he backed up against a beam. "I—General—sssir, am I dismissed?"

The general threw Tom a salute. "Yes, sir. As you were, mister. Dismissed."

Tom let out a pent-up breath, looked set to faint from relief.

"But, one thing. Don't ever leave without saying good-bye!"

Without warning, the general drew his Colt revolver, laughing wildly. Other renegade soldiers drew revolvers while others jacked the levers on Winchester rifles. Tom screamed.

A furious barrage of weapons fire shattered the ex-judge's scream. Dozens of bullets ripped Tom apart, the wall of lead pinning him to the beam, shearing him open, his skull exploding, his guts spewing everywhere. Through the din of weapons fire, Ki heard General Misery and his men laughing as they kept pumping lead into Tom. Finally, what was left of Tom the ex-judge pitched sideways in a torn and bloody heap.

Clouds of acrid gunsmoke wafted across the room. Ki was ready to leap into action as laughing eyes turned his way. Empty shell casings clattered to the floor as General Misery reloaded his revolver.

But, once again, General Misery picked out another target. Slowly, the General walked up behind Benny, the one-armed, one-eyed soldier.

His southern accent was purposely exaggerated as General Misery, holstering his still-smoking Colt, asked Benny, "I'm curious. How did you lose that arm and the eye, mister?"

Benny swallowed hard, not looking the general in the eye.

"Say something, damn you!"

"I—lost them in the War."

"A Yankee. A hero, I bet." The general grinned. "You lost an arm and an eye, but you people won. Oh, well. That's the way it goes, Yankee. Hey, I'm a fair man, a decent man, a good sport. You win some, you lose some. What the hell. As you were, soldier."

Benny looked relieved, as the general turned away. Benny raised the bottle of whiskey to his lips just as the General whirled and drove the saber clean through Benny's arm. An ear-shattering scream ripped from Benny's mouth as his arm thudded to the floor.

The general stepped back, his eyes glowing, clearly enjoying the pain and horror and the sight of Benny's blood spurting through the air from the stump of his upper arm.

As Benny turned, his one eye bulging in agony and rage, the general calmly stepped forward and drove his saber through Benny's good eye, silencing his screams.

One of the whores vomited.

Ki's breath felt like fire in his throat. He knew all of them were going to die after several long hours of torture, rape, and murder. He only hoped Jessie wasn't found. He told himself, *If this is the end, then so be it. Perhaps*, he thought, *both Jessie and I have lived long enough as it is.*

Blood-dripping blade by his side, General Misery, smiling, said, "Okay, let's have a party. We need pussy heat, we need love. And, hey, everything today, Bullshit there, he says it's on the house."

Jessie had heard the shooting, the screaming, and the sounds of wild laughter from evil men. She hustled Billy across the street, through the mist, and into the hotel. She found an empty room. She told Billy, "Stay here. No matter what happens, stay here."

Billy looked at Jessie fearfully. "Jessie, don't go. They'll kill you. Or worse."

"I have Ki to think of."

"So, this is Billy Johnson."

Jessie whirled, startled. Barabbas stood in the doorway with an odd grin on his face.

"Who are you?" Billy asked.

"He's nobody," Jessie said, staring Barabbas in the eye. "You sneak out of there?"

"If you're suggesting I'm a coward, lady, you can forget it. In fact, I'm ready when you are to make a grand entrance."

"Fifty thousand, huh? Like you said—if you live to spend it."

Barabbas cast Billy one last look. Jessie saw the flicker of greed in the bounty hunter's eyes. She knew where this was headed.

"Let's go," she told Barabbas. Then, at the door, she looked back at Billy. "Stay, Billy."

Billy looked set to say something, but Jessie shut the door, led Barabbas out of the hotel, and crossed the street.

From her saddle scabbard she unsheathed her Winchester rifle. Bullwhip around her shoulder, rifle in hand, she crouched beside the plate-glass window of Hell. She looked inside. What she saw didn't even really horrify her anymore. She had seen so much brutality and death here, she wondered if her soul had died altogether. *Oh, the last vestiges of humanity,* she thought, *where are you?*

She peered through the glass, Barabbas breathing down her neck. She saw Ki at their table, unharmed, watching General Misery and his soldiers at work.

The whores were being pumped by laughing, wild-eyed men. The whores were slapped, forced to swallow orgasms, taken up the ass, beaten bloody and senseless. Jessie saw Bull, also unharmed, but sitting there with murder in his eyes. It was only a matter of time before things erupted, she knew.

The whore, Donna, was passed around and raped by every last one of General Misery's men. When they were through with her, a gunshot rang out and Donna crumpled in a heap, her skull a bloody shattered thing. Then, General Misery, zipping himself up, roared, "God damn it, don't anybody kill another of these sluts! At this rate, they'll all be dead. Then what? We screw the Injun? Next one that kills a whore answers to me personally. I hope, by God, that I just made myself perfectly clear."

They began some serious drinking. Whores were made to stretch out and lie at the feet of the soldiers. One of the soldiers did something that almost made Bull snap.

The soldier took one of The Painter's works off the wall, sneered, "What is this shit?" and pissed all over it.

Bull stood.

"You got a problem?" General Misery barked.

Bull seemed to think better than to blow up with rage. "I need a drink."

"It's getting cold out here, lady."

Jessie looked over her shoulder at Barabbas. "I'm going to tell you something. Listen good. I saw the way you looked at Billy. I suggest you put it out of your mind."

"Put what?"

"You know what I'm talking about."

Suddenly, a situation developed in Hell. Jessie heard cursing and whooping. She saw that the soldiers had discovered the tub of filth.

"What is this?" General Misery asked, looming over the swimmers in shit. "Now, ain't this a sight! Hey, Injun, this ain't a bad touch. Lemme guess here. You get upset with someone, you dump them in shit. Not bad. I like it. In fact, I like it so much, how 'bout I give you a taste here. Stand up!"

Jessie saw Bull visibly tense with fear.

"This is it, Barabbas," Jessie growled, standing.

Without warning, the renegade soldiers surrounded Bull. Bull broke jaws, snapped an arm like a twig, fought, and bellowed, but he was finally pummeled to the floor by fists and rifle butts. They dragged him toward the tub.

Jessie opened the door and walked into Hell.

★

Chapter 13

With the stench of blood, guts, and shit in her nose, Jessie stood inside the doorway, Barabbas beside her. Just as they were about to dump Bull in shit, they all looked her way. She stood, still as a statue, eyes hard, face grim, the Winchester canted to her shoulder.

They stared, leered, whistled, muttered, and scratched themselves.

Jessie smiled a cold, mean smile, having their full and undivided attention. This was her play, she knew. For some reason, she was primed to end it here, one way or another. Billy was alive and safe. No matter what, he could just ride on out. Maybe write some epic poem about the Lone Star Legend, Jessie thought, and a big Indian named Bull.

"I have one question for all of you. Are you men

or are you boys?" Jessie laughed, then slipped off her coat, unbuttoned her blouse, and let a creamy breast hang out, the nipple swollen and rigid. "Why don't you drop the Indian and come here, let me see what you've got?"

They looked at each other, uncertain, smiles nervous.

Jessie cupped her breast, ran her tongue over her lips. "Come on."

General Misery nodded at three of his men. They dropped Bull in a bloody heap in front of the tub.

With cautious steps, three of the renegades walked toward Jessie, their eyes alight with wild lust.

"That's right, come closer," Jessie said in a sweet, seductive voice. "Pull it out, let me see what you've got. All three of you. Come on, don't be bashful."

They stopped, several feet short of Jessie.

"Oh, fellas, this will be sweet," said one of them, a tobacco-chewer with red eyes and whiskey breath so strong it was all Jessie could do to keep from gagging.

One by one, they unzipped themselves, let it fall out.

Jessie frowned, then laughed, long and hard. "Like I thought. You're boys. How pitiful. How do you please a woman with that? Look at the three of you, you're disgusting. You stand there, grinning like idiots, like you've got somethin' worth grinnin' about."

They reached for iron. Very stupid thing to do.

"Why, you—you bitch!"

The Winchester swept down, Jessie cupped the barrel in her hand, and shot the guy in the face. As he tumbled backward, Jessie jacked the lever twice, shot the other two in the crotch, blowing off what little was there.

Everyone just froze.

Mindless screaming filled the silence.

Then all hell broke loose.

Ki jumped to his feet, hurling one, then two throwing stars across the room. Skulls cracked, as the *shuriken* embedded themselves into temples, causing instant twitching death. General Misery and his flunkies had been so brazen, they had not even bothered to disarm anyone in the saloon.

Bad mistake.

It became a deadly free-for-all, every man and woman for themselves.

Bull came to full vengeful life. He reached between the legs of a Confederate flunkie, grabbed his balls, and squeezed. The guy howled in mindless agony, before Bull wrenched and pulled back a bloody handful of balls and pitched them into the shit.

The two Jessie had shot in the package wailed, on and on, but the furious din of revolvers, rifle fire, and whores shrieking in terror drowned out their howls.

Side by side, Jessie and Barabbas stood their ground, blazing away with rifles.

Ki's sword flashed, cleaved off a head, and sent it twirling through the air.

Bull punched, kicked, and flailed, crushing faces and skulls with his hands and feet, hurling lifeless sacks in all directions. He was every bit the rampaging bull, bellowing, snorting, killing with his bare hands. It was a fearsome sight, this giant of a man smashing skulls together, snapping arms and necks like matchsticks, moving so fast he was a blur.

Stacey went to work with her whip. She flailed some guy to his knees, then wrapped her whip around this renegade's throat, tied him to a beam, kneed him in the balls, and slapped him silly for a few seconds. Jessie caught a glimpse of this action, then it hit her that this was the pisser and it had been Stacey's portrait he had desecrated. As the pisser struggled, his eyes wide with fear, his mouth trying to work to blubber for mercy, the whores descended on him. Knives flashed, shredding the man to bloody meat within seconds. Stacey freed him, and, as he crumpled at her feet, moaning and crying, Stacey squatted over him.

"Piss on me, will ya?" Stacey laughed, and returned the favor.

The regular gunmen joined the savage fight. Their weapons blazed. Scissored between the whores, the patrons of Hell, Bull, Jessie, Ki, and Barabbas, the renegade soldiers dropped in screaming, bloody piles.

Like cradling a baby in his arms, Bull lifted one renegade high in the air, then slammed the guy over his knee. The renegade's spine snapped like a twig. Bull flung him away like he weighed no more than a feather.

General Misery swung his saber, fired his Colt, lashing at anything and everything, skewering and shooting several of his own men in a blind panic. The general stumbled, nosedived, then began crawling for cover behind the bar.

Naked whores, smelling blood, insane with rage and vengeance, snatched up rifles and revolvers. With deadly cool, they walked toward the renegades, firing away. Return fire blasted three of the whores off their feet, but the whores braved death to dish it out. When two of them reached the ball-less ones, squirming around in their blood like maggots in garbage, they shot them in the face.

Jessie angled across the saloon, picking out targets with steely calm, dropping them where they stood.

There was much screaming and wailing for mercy from the renegades. There was much suffering and terrible dying.

The end for them could not have come soon enough.

Jessie watched, as Bull thundered two big paws into the backside of General Misery. Terror in his eyes, the general looked up at Bull.

"Let's take a swim!" Bull roared, lifting the general off his feet, snatching the saber out of his hand. With a vicious backhand, Bull dropped General Misery on his back, then broke the saber over his knee and tossed it away.

With sword and revolver, Ki helped the whores and Barabbas finish off the renegades, guys spinning, screaming, and falling all over the saloon, gutted by blade, blown apart by lead, blinded by whips, devoured by whores who ripped out throats with bare hands.

Jessie fanned the saloon, searching for targets. No one appeared left alive but General Misery.

Bull hauled General Misery off his feet, head-butted him, crushing his nose. Bull slammed the general to the floor, kicked him in the face. He released the Confederate general and loomed over him. General Misery, head bent, was bleeding and coughing.

Bull looked at several of his whores. "You finish him. In the tub. Enjoy. You earned it."

The naked whores swooped down on General Misery.

Jessie held her ground, watching this fearsome display of vengeance, as the whores dragged a blubbering General Misery toward the tub.

"No, no—no!" the general pleaded, as the whores forced him over the edge, dunking his face in the filth and holding him there. His legs kicked with fury for several moments, his arms flailing, filth spraying the whores, all of them gritting their teeth, cursing, but keeping him forced in the filth, drowning him. Finally, his legs still, the general was dumped in the filth.

The whores shut the closet door.

A groan.

Several groans.

Jessie saw some of the dead weren't dead. Bellowing, Bull walked up to a renegade soldier, lifted his foot and stomped on the guy's neck. There was a sickening crack of bone.

Two other groaners were sheared apart by a hail of rifle and revolver fire. Stacey was pissed because she wanted them for herself. She found one, still alive, and used her whip to beat him to death.

In the long moments of hard and awful silence that followed, Jessie just stood there, looking at Ki through the drifting clouds of gunsmoke.

There was a celebration of sorts following the slaughter of General Misery and his misfits.

There was also another problem to deal with.

Jessie, sitting beside Ki, watching the whores drinking and smoking and congratulating each other with hugs, kisses, and fondling, drank from a fresh bottle. Bull ordered the dead to be tossed out into the street.

This was where new trouble started.

Several of the gunmen tried to appear casual, as they helped remove the dead. But Jessie sensed their greed, knew what they were.

When the last of the dead were tossed out into the street, Bull, moving to the window, discovered what was happening.

Bull grunted. Bottle and gun in hand, he walked outside.

Jessie followed Bull out into the street. There, several gunmen were checking the renegade soldiers, leafing through wanted posters.

"Problem?" Bull growled.

The bounty hunters looked at Bull, afraid. One of them reached for a gun, and Bull shot him in the head.

Through the mist, Barabbas arrived in his large buckboard.

" 'Preciate the thoughtfulness, Bull," Barabbas said, stopping his buckboard in front of the dead, his revolver already drawn and pointed at Bull. Swinging his aim, Barabbas shot the three other bounty hunters in the head: No sooner was their blood spraying the snow, than Barabbas had cocked and pointed the gun at Bull again.

Jessie and Ki stood beside Bull. Bull drank, kept his revolver low by his side.

"Toss the gun away, Bull," Barabbas ordered in a flat, bored voice.

Bull tossed the gun away, looking every bit as bored as Barabbas sounded. "Help yourself."

Barabbas looked confused, then scared for a second. "I almost think you mean that."

"I do. Indeed, when you're finished loading that shit, come on in. Jane will let you have a fresh bottle. No, on second thought, take all you need. On the house."

Barabbas peered at Bull, suspicious. "Thanks, but, no thanks. I'll just load up and be on my way."

"I insist."

Barabbas locked Bull's mean-eyed stare.

"I insist. Do not leave here without accepting my hospitality. I would be much insulted."

Barabbas shrugged. "Okay. If you insist. Thanks."

"You're welcome."

And Bull went into Hell.

Jessie watched as Barabbas loaded the dead into his buckboard. It took him a good thirty minutes to pile the dead up. Grunting and groaning through it all, Barabbas glared at Jessie and Ki. Jessie just watched.

When he was finished, Jessie said, "I think you'd just better leave town. Now. You got what you want. You'll be a rich man. Congratulations."

"Hey, I intend to leave town. But you heard Bull. A most hospitable feller, I must say. Think I'll help myself to his booze, after all," the bounty hunter said, stepping up on the boardwalk. "Maybe three, four bottles, to get me through the rest of the winter. If you'll excuse me."

Jessie stepped aside. She sensed something was up, and believed either Barabbas was a fool, or he thought he was in control. Bull did not just let a man walk away, having his way.

Jessie followed Barabbas inside. She looked at Ki, who said nothing.

They waited.

Barabbas searched the saloon. There was no sign of Bull.

"Hey, uh, Jane," Barabbas called out.

"Yeah, I know. Bull told me. How many bottles you want?"

Barabbas must have begun to sense something was wrong. He took several long moments to look around at the whores. All of them just sat there in the saloon, some looking hard-eyed, others grinning.

"I'll be fair," Barabbas said. "Hey, I'm not a greedy man, I'm not one to take advantage. Give me—ah, say five bottles. Throw in a couple of steaks while you're at it."

141

Jane smiled at some of the whores.

Barabbas dropped his hand over his gun butt. "Easy, baby, easy."

"Hey, come on, mister," Jane said in a calm voice. "No tricks here. You can have your whiskey, the steaks, too. I'll be glad to give it to you. Then you can be on your way." Jane put five bottles on the bar and added two big packages of steak.

"What the fuck is going on here?" Barabbas growled.

Silence.

Then Jessie smelled something, whiffed the air. It was a smell of kerosene, then of roasting flesh. She heard the crackle of flames, saw the shadows of fire dancing through the window, over the saloon.

She whirled toward the doorway, the same instant that Barabbas screamed, "Noooooo!!"

And Barabbas ran out into the street.

"You rotten pig!" Barabbas screamed.

Jessie barreled through the door, then stopped beside a horrified Barabbas.

"Noooooo!!!"

Bull, grinning, stepped away from the hearse that was now engulfed in flames. Bull pitched the empty kerosene bucket away, his revolver low by his side. He motioned with his hand at Barabbas, four other large empty kerosene buckets scattered around the giant Indian. "Come on, bounty hunter. Do it."

Barabbas seethed in silence as he watched his fortune going up in flames.

Behind her, Jessie heard the whores laughing,

then some of the women clapped and congratulated Bull.

"Yeah, take that in, why don't you," Bull said, jerking a nod at the burning dead. "Yeah, bounty hunter, I can hear you now. 'But, I'm telling you, that's General Misery and his men. They're worth fifty grand! Don't you believe me?'"

And Bull roared with laughter.

Indeed, everyone laughed but Barabbas, who staggered toward the bonfire and looked ready to weep.

"Now," Bull chuckled, glancing back at the flaming hearse, "that, I believe, is what they call dreams going up in smoke."

As Bull stepped past Barabbas, watching the bounty hunter out of the corner of his eye, Jessie smiled.

Bull said to Jessie, "Are you my woman now? My diamond?"

Jessie's smile widened as Barabbas roared with rage, hit his knees, and looked like he was going to rip his hair out with his hands.

"You bet I am, stud," Jessie chuckled as Barabbas screamed his rage. "I'm all yours."

★

Chapter 14

Following the incident of the flaming hearse, nothing much happened. Jessie spent a long, hard, and, at times, painful night with Bull and slept well into the next morning. When she awoke, she found Bull asleep, snoring lightly, his pole hard and sticking more than halfway up his belly, damn near resting on his chest. No doubt, she thought, he had a mean piss hard-on. Sore, raw, and groggy, Jessie was not up to taking that thing in her again. Quietly, she took a bath, spending a good hour in the tub, relaxing, knowing that Billy was back in his room, safe and sound. Later, she decided she would try one last time to persuade the boy to leave this town, turn himself over to the law, take his chances. Jessie would hire the best attorney she could find for him. But, she decided she would let Billy make the call.

Dressed, feeling better, she went out into the

saloon. The place was empty, except for Barabbas. Her mood turned sour at the sight of the bounty hunter.

As if to taunt him a little, smiling to herself, she walked to the door. There was nothing left of the buckboard now but a pile of ashes, nothing left of the dead but charred, unrecognizable ruins.

"Yeah, that's right, grin and chuckle; rub it in."

Jessie turned and looked the bounty hunter in the eye.

Barabbas scratched a match off the tabletop, fired up, sipped some whiskey. He was bleary-eyed, half drunk, reeking of whiskey and sweat.

He looked and sounded bored as he said, "That was it, lady, that was the dumbest damn move anyone has ever pulled on me. Cheap, dirty move. Then you walk off hand in hand with the big stud. Like I give a damn you're screwing him, like it's really going to hurt me. You stupid bitch."

Jessie steeled herself.

"Whiskey?" Barabbas offered, his smile mean.

"No, thanks. I think today I'll stay sober."

"Screw you," he grumbled.

"No, thanks, my dance card's filled."

Barabbas snorted. "So, how is he? How's it feel to take that big piece of buck meat up your pussy? Go down on it, too? I bet you did. Damn whore," he grumbled.

Jessie was a heartbeat away from walking across the room and slapping the hell out of the bounty hunter. Instead, she just smiled at Barabbas.

"I'd ask you why you're hanging around here still, but I think I already know," she told him.

"Oh? Why's that?"

"You don't want to leave here empty-handed. Your pride won't let you. Word of warning: Don't let your pride get you killed."

"Don't you worry about my pride, lady."

Barabbas stood, grabbed up his bottle, and moved to the door.

"Your buddy, he's been standing outside now for about an hour."

Jessie peered through the door. Like Barabbas said, she found Ki standing alone on the other side of the street, a mere dark shadow in the thick mist.

"Looks like I'm not the only one around here a little unhappy with you," Barabbas said, then left, walking across the street, angling for the hotel.

Jessie felt her heart grow heavy as she stood there, staring at Ki, who looked so small, so alone and troubled. She walked across the street.

"Ki?"

Slowly, he turned, his eyes full of sorrow.

Silence, heavy and hard and painful.

Jessie stared at this man, a man she had known for so long, who had protected her and saved her life, who would die for her without hesitation. She touched his face, a tear welling up in the corner of her eye.

Ki was still, his face soft and tender.

"Ki—oh, Ki." Jessie swallowed hard. "I am sorry I have hurt you. Forgive me. I love you, I will never hurt you again. Believe me, please, I am so very sorry."

Ki looked disturbed for a moment, his stare haunted.

Jessie froze, wanting to ask him what was wrong. Ki breathed hard for a moment, looked set to collapse.

"Ki? Are you all right? What is it?"

Ki swallowed hard, then smiled. "Jessie— Jessie—"

Ki took Jessie in his arms. They embraced for a long time, just stood there, holding each other.

When they returned to their table, Jessie and Ki quietly played poker, sitting in comfortable silence. As the hours dragged on, Jessie became depressed. She fought these feelings, the anger that had been inside her for so long, that swollen fire in the belly Bull had mentioned. Would these feelings ever pass?

Ki noticed her torment. "Are you all right, Jessie?"

She smiled, touched his hand. "I'm really not sure, Ki."

"I know I've been after you about your attitude, lately. I just care, that's all."

"I know you do. I—I guess I just haven't wanted you to care. You're too close to me, you know me too well. When I suffer, you suffer, too. And the other way around. I need to live again, Ki, I need a reason to live."

"You have one, right now: Billy. Be patient, I caught a glimpse of the boy as you and Bull brought him back here. He's young, but I see the pain he's felt in his eyes. Give him time, give him room to breathe. He'll come around."

"Or he won't."

Ki shrugged. "You can only try. That is your reason to live—to try." Sighing, Ki stood, went to the bar, brought back a bottle of whiskey. He took a drink, handed the bottle to Jessie.

Jessie smiled at Ki, took the bottle, sipped. A moment later, the warm glow spread inside her. She felt just a little better. Not much better.

"It's okay," Ki told her. "See, there are some things I, too, have come to understand. What we want cannot be denied. It is, perhaps, even wrong to deny what we want. Take what you want in life, Jessie. A man, a drink, whatever. Only you have to answer to yourself. Not me, not anyone here in the world, in the flesh. You have a good heart, a beautiful heart, and it will always shine through, no matter what. I have seen changes in you that are frightening to me, but I stood by and watched. What else could I do? We all must walk a dark path at some point in our lives. A life that is lived without being scarred is not worth living."

Jessie showed Ki a warm smile. "It sounds like you learned a lot from Cassandra."

"I cannot tell you at this point what I learned. I don't even know. But I caught a fleeting glimpse of the future, or some of the future."

"She has that kind of power; I know, I felt it."

"I have to believe, I have to have faith that things will be made right. Here and beyond. For us. For Billy. I know your pain, I have seen it every day. What has gone before us must be left in the past. All we have is now."

"And each other."

"Yes. And each other."

What was left of the happy hour crew wandered in toward evening. Jason, Rufus, and Pete sat brooding in dismal silence. They looked haunted, still shaken by the events of yesterday. Jessie felt compassion for them. She stood and walked to the bar. They looked at her, uncertain, afraid.

"I look at you and I wonder why you stay here," Jessie said.

Rufus grunted, said, "I don't know why I stay here. I guess—there's nothing left for me—no place for any of us to go."

"You're feeling sorry for yourselves," Jessie said in a soft voice. "I don't mean that in an unkind way. But staying in this place of death is pointless."

Pete said, "Maybe not."

"How so?" Jessie asked.

"Yeah, we're feeling sorry for ourselves, all right. Damn, but strange as it sounds, I'm almost sorry I wasn't killed yesterday. Sure, what the hell, while I'm feeling sorry, I might as well get it all out. See, I used to have big dreams. That big book I was going to write. Never going to happen. Why? I don't deserve anything good, I am unworthy. You know, Bull was right. I, we here, we do nothing but talk, dream, bullshit. Thing is, you get older, you lose steam, you don't care anymore. I see the way you look at us, we're losers to you, and, hey, you're right. I came to this town with nothing, and I will leave this world less than nothing. You know why? I'll tell you why, I'll tell you what we are. We're cowards. I watched the people here die, right in that church, massacred for no damn good reason. I'm a coward, because I hid, watched them die, in fact, from a safe distance. So did Jason, Bernie, Tom, and Rufus. And, yes, even the war hero, he watched them die. Scared shitless to try and stop it. All of the people rounded up, marched into that church, and burned to death. Women and children, screaming—God, I have nightmares about it. The ones who tried to escape, they were gunned down as they ran out of the church, trying to flee from the fire."

What compassion Jessie had dredged up for them disappeared, replaced by contempt and revulsion.

"Yeah, we are some sorry assholes," Jason said, sullen. "Just because we didn't have family ourselves—we watched it all happen. We're just as guilty as the ones who murdered them."

"Maybe even more so," Rufus added. "So we drink to kill the pain and the memories and the mere thought of our own cowardice. We sit here, slowly committing suicide by drinking hard and heavy every day, waiting for our turn."

Jessie shook her head, utterly disgusted.

"Would you like to shoot us now and just get it over with?" Rufus suggested with a self-mocking smile.

"Would you be terribly offended if I told you you're not even worth shooting?" Jessie said.

"Not at all," Rufus replied.

"Why were they murdered?" Jessie wanted to know.

Rufus shrugged. "Who knows? Just because they were there. Who knows why evil men do evil? To them, it was like some great accomplishment, some mark of pride. And the ones who did it, many of them stayed on, hell, you see them here every day."

Jessie was almost afraid to ask her next question, but she had to know. "And Bull? Was he here when it happened?"

"No."

Jessie felt a strange sense of relief.

Rufus went on. "Bull showed up about a month later. One big badass buck Injun with his band of beautiful whores. Big pimp, rode in to make a buck. Lots of takers. Had plenty of booze, hell, he had three buckboards heaped with beer and whiskey and steaks. He was treated like royalty. Course, he had to kill a few guys who got out of line, just to show everyone he was in charge."

"When he heard the story of what happened to the people here," Pete said, "Bull changed. Everyone who stayed could expect the worst. That's when he implemented the tub of shit, told us all that's what we were, just shit. He's right. We're shit."

Jessie felt exhausted all of a sudden. Shaking her head, she walked away from them, fully intending to not even acknowledge their sorry existence the rest of the time she was in Hell.

★

Chapter 15

Jessie and Ki sat in silence at their usual table in Hell for some time. Neither Barabbas nor Bull were anywhere to be found. She didn't trust Barabbas out of her sight, and she fretted over Bull's state of mind about The Painter, wanting to be with him, but feeling it best if she left him alone.

Late in the afternoon, Jessie stood, told Ki she was going to talk to Billy, that she'd be back shortly, and she'd let him know what they were going to do.

She knocked on Bull's door, told him it was her.

Inside, she found Bull stretched out on his bed, naked, a bottle of whiskey in his hand, a strange haunted look in his eyes. Bull's cheeks were wet from tears.

"You do not need to knock, white woman. My room is yours."

"Okay."

"Lay with for me awhile."

"Bull—"

"Lay! Please. I know you are sore and tired and that you have had many orgasms and do not need Bull's cock right now. I do not want that right now, anyway. Must I ask you again to lay with me?"

"No."

"Later maybe, after Bull rests, his big balls will be full for you and I will give you what it is you want."

"Don't talk to me like that. Like a whore. Please."

Bull chuckled, but said, "Very good. Forgive me."

She stretched out beside Bull, draped a leg over his belly. She felt his body shudder with suppressed, quiet sobs. Sighing, she took Bull's head in her arms, cradling his face to her bosom. For a good hour she held him.

"You can go to the boy. I decided it's best he leave," Bull said. "If you cannot persuade my young William, I will tell him he must go. There is life for him somewhere. The rest of us—I had a dream last night. I saw fire. I saw death. I saw blood, much blood and fire. The end is upon us, Most Beautiful of White Women. It will be a very terrible end for all of us."

"Bull, you can leave here anytime you want. You don't have to die."

Bull snorted. "Why do you think I called this place Hell? It was I who renamed the town also. It all fits. I have read your white people's words from the Great One, many many times. Bull reads much. Bull is no dummy."

"I know that. In your own way, Bull, you're a genius."

"I believe you mean that. Thank you. Go now to the boy. I need to sleep. I—I need to pray, also."

"Pray?"

"Yes. Pray. It is strange, but inside, I believe one can know when death is coming. One must prepare. Some must prepare to die more than others, for their wrongdoing is greater and He Who Watches and Knows All, He is much unhappy with Bull and the miserable sorry lot of unworthy ones I am surrounded with. Bull's wrong has been great, so great I fear the Great One—I fear the Great One. I am unworthy, so unworthy, I am not fit to even take my own life, I must die after great suffering to cleanse my black soul. Bull, he would never beg or ask any man for a thing. With the Great One it will be different. I will plead for forgiveness at His feet."

Jessie stared at Bull, her heart heavy with sorrow. For some reason, looking into his eyes, Jessie sensed death about this man, too.

"Go, white woman."

Jessie went to Billy.

She found Billy, drunk, with pen and pad in hand.

Billy didn't look up at Jessie. "I heard what he said."

"Then you know he's right."

"I know no such thing."

"Billy. You can come back to the ranch with Ki and me. I will protect you, you will want for nothing."

"You will, huh? How about other things?"

"What other—Billy, no, I already told you about that."

"I'm too young, right? I'm twenty-one, Jessie. I'm a man."

"Yes. In your own way, you are. But there is a lot you must learn about life."

Billy drank long and hard. He let out a string of vicious cursing. He looked demonic to Jessie.

It was no use trying to reason with him, Jessie saw now. He was surly and belligerent, frustrated, afraid, and angry.

"I tell you what, Jessie, tomorrow I'll give you an answer—tomorrow sometime. Let me finish this poem."

"Very good. I'll wait. Tomorrow, Billy. One way or another, I'm leaving tomorrow."

"Whatever."

Jessie left, frustrated, afraid, and angry herself. Bull was sound asleep, snoring away. She took his bottle from him. He'd had enough to drink and as for more sex, she'd make him wait. She was feeling mean and surly herself. The day was still young and all she wanted right then was to get good and drunk and forget. Everyone there thought they were so goddamn smart, she thought, going out into the saloon, finding the happy hour crew not so happy, the gunmen wittled down to maybe a dozen, looking mean and surly and tight. Damn them all. Bull was right. None of them were worth a shit, and she had the urge to rage at all of them, to reduce them to shit with a stream of verbal venom.

Ki asked her, "What happened with the kid? You don't look too happy."

"I'm all right, Ki. With you, things are all right now. With the rest of them, I'm just about ready to give up and ride out. One more day. We give it one more day. Billy's going to play his spoiled, spurned little boy game. I'll let it ride."

"He wants you."

"But I don't want him. Not that way."

"You feel like a mother to him."

"No. More like a sister. A sister who might put his little ass over my knee and make him beg for mercy."

Ki smiled. "You know something? Whatever changes you've gone through—by God, sometimes, when you talk like that—you're beautiful."

Jessie laughed. "You know something, I think you're exactly right about that. Tell me just how beautiful I am. Stroke my ego and make me feel good."

"All right. Here goes—"

Night came. The kerosene light washed over the inhabitants of Hell in a dull, flickering sheen that made all of them look ghostly in their perfect isolation, as the whores, Bull, the regulars, the gunmen, Jessie, Ki, and Barabbas sat in brooding silence, smoking, drinking, and looking just generally miserable and lost and lonely.

What they waited for was death. Jessie felt it in the air, now more than ever. *Oh, death,* she thought, *when will you come? Come soon, please. Spare none of us. Make us weep, make us suffer, make us die, long and hard and angry.* All of them, she knew, were far beyond the final, tired, clinging phase.

Jessie heard the soft clopping of horse hooves. She strained to make out the figure riding toward the window of the saloon. At first, she thought no one was riding the scrawniest, ugliest black pony she'd ever seen. Then she made out a figure on the pony that was so small that she thought it was a child.

Everyone waited for the figure to come into Hell. The door opened. He stood there, slapping the snow off his body.

Jessie could not believe what she saw as she strained to make out the odd figure through the haze and cigar and cigarette smoke.

It was not a boy, but a man with a soft, chubby, cherubic face, standing maybe four and a half feet tall. The tiny man wore a weird grin, with a wild light in his eyes. He was wearing a white, ten-gallon hat, with a white coat about five sizes too big. His arms and legs nowhere to be found until he hitched up his sleeves and slapped some snow off his hat.

"Hear ye, hear ye," the midget announced, grinning at everyone in the saloon. "May I kindly have the attention of all gathered!" His voice was like that of some hysterical woman, high-pitched, squeaking, strained. Suddenly, he giggled, tittered, grinned, then he rubbed his ass. He frowned, then shuddered, looking like he was trying to compose himself.

A heavy expectant hush filled the saloon.

"Ladies and gentlemen, allow me to introduce myself. I am called Tinker Bell, sometimes known as Twinkle Toes, sometimes referred to as Greasy Cheeks or the Mouth Fairy." He giggled. "Get it? Mouth Fairy?" Tinker Bell giggled. "I have a most important announcement to make. It concerns your future. I have been sent ahead by them who are everything terrible in life. You will heed this warning. There are four of them. They are war, death, famine, and plague. They are also known as the Four Horsemen. You will pay them homage, you will give them your honor and respect, lest you upset them and cause yourselves terrible suffering. Now, this is what I come to say unto you. There is a young boy, a very pretty young boy who writes poetry. This young boy killed a trollop back East. They who are fearsome to all and forgiving to none know the pretty young boy is here. Now, pay careful attention, Tinker Bell is not one to repeat himself. They who are forgiving to none, they will let you live, but you must turn the pretty young boy over to them when they arrive. I will not say that they will come like thieves in the night, but they will come. When, you will not know. You have been warned. That is all. I, the Mouth Fairy, also known as Tinker Bell, Twinkle Toes, and Greasy Cheeks, I bid you fond adieu."

Giggling, the midget with many names waddled up to the bar and climbed up onto a barstool. He peeled off some money. "A bottle of whiskey, kind lady."

Jane just stared at the Mouth Fairy, then looked at Bull, who grunted and nodded. Jane gave the midget the bottle, swiped up the money. Without another word, the midget waddled out of the saloon, climbed up a ladder attached to his pony, then rode off into the night.

For some time, no one said a word.

Jessie felt the fear in the saloon, and she saw the fear in Bull's eyes. She locked his gaze, thinking, *What in the world was that all about?*

Finally, Bull stood, came toward her table. He did not look happy.

★

Chapter 16

Bull just stood beside their table, staring at them, haunted. Jessie looked from Bull to Ki. The big Indian and her half-breed protector stared at each other, making her wonder if they knew something she didn't.

"It is as I have seen," Bull said. "The dream—indeed, I believe it was no dream, it was a prophecy. What I saw—I saw a white haze—a woman in black—I believe she had no eyes. She looked at me, I was right there beside her, this woman with black dress and white eyes, this woman I have never seen before. What I believe, I believe she showed me the future. I did not tell you this, O, Beautiful One, this part of the dream, the prophecy. I saw them, the four." For a terrible moment, Bull was silent. Then he continued, "Bull, he has heard of these men. It is said they have killed more than a thousand men for blood money, that they are rich, that they claim to have more money than the Great One. That they are mean and quick as a rattlesnake with a gun. We have much to fear, even though they are only four, they will be more fearsome and terrible than the shit my whores killed in the shit."

"I have heard of the Four Horsemen," Jessie said, "but not recently, and not much. I thought they were some—myth."

"As in the words of the Great One," Bull went on, "they steal their identity from the Book of Revelation. They believe they cleanse the world of evil. They are no myth. This is why perhaps you have not heard much about them. Do you see, they are so feared, I hear, that no one speaks of them, believing they will be killed in the night by them. They are like ghosts when they kill. Silent, swift, these men, they kill in the dark, come when you do not expect them."

Jessie was silent for a long moment, then said, "Well, I guess there's nothing for us to do—but wait for them."

And wait and worry they did.

The Four Horsemen, they who were terrible to all and forgiving to none, did not come like thieves that night, nor well into the next morning.

Jessie did not sleep that night. After pleasing Bull, she fell asleep sometime early the next morning. When she awoke, she discovered it was late in the afternoon.

More white mist. More grim silence in the saloon.

Someone reported seeing Barabbas, wandering in the mist. Then the bounty hunter vanished into the hotel.

After a late meal of steak, Jessie was ready for the day. She went to Billy's room.

Billy seemed terribly sad. He moaned "Jessie—Jessie—will you hold me?"

Jessie held him.

"Jessie—I'm sorry—the things I said. The way I am sometimes, it's not me. I can't explain. Will you forgive me?"

"Yes. Of course, Billy."

He pulled back, smiled at her, then he became grim. "Jessie—I am young, I know, but I understand something, something very sad, something very awful. This is a truth of life. This is the truth I have discovered, this is why I say the world is on fire. The truth is, the world does not care whether you live or die. When you understand this and accept it, this awful truth of life, you become free in a way, but also you become trapped and afraid." With a grim smile, he said, "Listen to me, will ya, I'm starting to talk like Bull."

Jessie swallowed hard, thinking of her own pain, her own losses, those rare and fleeting moments in life when all is well and good, moments that vanish all too quickly.

"Yes, Billy, I believe that, too. But you are right, and you are wrong. The world does not care if you live or die, but you must care, and there are those few, close to you, family and a few friends who care. Beyond that, it is all loneliness and isolation and fear."

163

Billy seemed to think about this. He nodded. "Listen—I want to go with you, but, please, understand, give me some time, maybe another day or two. My poem is almost finished. Can you wait? Will you?"

Jessie smiled. "Two more days—at the most. Finish your poem."

She kissed him on the cheek.

She stood, about to leave his room. Billy said, "Jessie?"

She turned, saw his eyes were wet with tears. Her heart sank.

"Jessie—thank you. It was me who hurt you. I did you wrong. I stole from you, I took advantage. I will never hurt you like that again. Say you forgive me? Right now, it's more important to me than anything else."

"I forgive you. Now, get to work on that poem."

One more smile, and Jessie left his room.

She went to her table where Ki waited.

Everyone waited in dread for the four who are terrible to all and forgiving to none.

They came three days after the midget had announced their arrival. It was dusk. The white mist was darkening as the sun set over Apocalypse.

Jessie had decided to search for Barabbas to tell him to get the hell out of town. She was walking across the street when she saw them. Jessie stopped in the middle of the street and peered into the mist, seeing their shapes roll up out of the white sheet to the east.

The Four Horsemen slowly rode into town. There was a black horse, a white horse, a pale dun horse, and, finally, a chestnut horse whose color was so red that for a moment Jessie wondered if the color was natural. Each rider wore a long coat and hat the color of his mount. The midget rode behind the four, a rope tied around his throat and attached the saddle horn of the black rider. As they approached the saloon, Jessie watched them closely. All of them were bearded but for the pale rider, whose skin was as white as snow. They did not even look her way until they pulled up in front of the saloon. Then they cast her a piercing look with eyes that appeared dead. They dismounted and tied the midget to a beam. The red rider forced the midget to his knees. The midget giggled his strange giggle.

The Four Horsemen, one by one, walked into Hell.

Jessie followed them inside and took her seat beside Ki.

Bull was there, along with the regulars, the whores, and the remaining gunmen. Silently, fearfully, everyone watched as the four bounty hunters walked to the bar. The white rider snapped his fingers and said, "Whiskey."

After looking at Bull, who grunted his okay, Jane got them a bottle.

Long moments of tense silence passed as everyone watched the four bounty hunters pass around the whiskey bottle and fire up cheroots. They smoked, flicking ashes all over the bar. When they drained the bottle, they ordered a fresh one, set up shot glasses, and slowed their pace.

The door opened.

The preacher walked in. He stopped in the middle of the room.

As if on cue, the four bounty hunters slowly pulled back their coats, draping their hands over their revolvers. They didn't look the preacher's way.

"You!" the preacher railed at the foursome. "You abomination! I know who you are! You call yourselves the Four Horsemen. You think you kill in the name of God! This is a terrible sin! Yes, I've heard of you! You cannot hide your abomination from God! Woe to you! Woe I say! You are a scourge, indeed, but you are full of evil!"

"Who, or what is that?" the pale rider asked no one in particular, his steely gaze fixed on his shot glass as he sipped whiskey.

There was no answer.

"Someone kindly answer my question before I become greatly annoyed," the pale rider said.

Rufus, shuffling away from them, croaked, "Th-that's—the preacher. Preacher Bob John."

The white rider smiled.

"You four are evil men. Just what we need— more evil in this already evil town. The Lord God will strike you all down! All of you must perish in the lake of fire. It is written!"

At the same time, the four chuckled. It was a grim, mean sound.

"You laugh at me! A man of God! How dare you!"

Before the preacher could continue, the red rider said, "Preacher! Be silent, be still. You are the gnat on a donkey's ass. I am a word away from swatting you and crushing you like the insect you are."

These words, edged with ice and menace, froze the Preacher.

"So—man of God," the red rider said, looking down into his shot glass, "I have one question to ask you. Feel free to be honest and straightforward. This is a moment of truth. This is what I ask you in the name of truth." Slowly, the red rider turned, his eyes filled with a wild light as he fixed the preacher with his penetrating stare. "Can your God, preacher man, save you from death?"

Several stretched seconds of utter silence.

The preacher's lips quivered. He stayed silent.

"As I thought," the red rider said, turning back to his whiskey.

"You—you—you abomination! All of you must die!" The preacher wheeled, then stormed out of the saloon.

Jessie, tense, kept her hand close to her holster.

"I will say this one time, and one time only," the pale rider said, again to no one in particular. "Hand the boy over to us. If you do, you will live. Do it now. We will give you two minutes to consider this most serious matter."

Two minutes of serious consideration passed. Bull, sitting on his divan, watched the four.

Finally, Bull said, "I believe two minutes are up. I do not see any boy you speak of."

"Very good, sir," the pale rider said. "We appreciate your consideration of this most serious matter. Thank you."

Slowly, they moved away from the bar. One by one, the Four Horsemen left Hell. Jessie watched as they untied the midget, marched across the street, and vanished into the hotel.

Bull went to his room to be close to young William.

Some of the whores went upstairs with gunmen. Even the prospect of impending doom and death did not disrupt business as usual.

Jessie was about to get up and go issue that ultimatum to the bounty hunter, when she heard a commotion in Bull's room.

Leaping to her feet, gun in hand, Jessie rushed to Bull's room with Ki beside her.

They found Bull in a heap beside his bed, blood trickling down the side of his face. Barabbas stood in the doorway to Billy's room. The bounty hunter tossed away the big, heavy stick that he's used to club Bull.

Jessie bent beside Bull. She found a pulse. When she looked up, she saw Barabbas pointing his revolver at her and Ki.

"You want to talk about dumb moves," Jessie said, taking a step toward Barabbas.

Barabbas cocked the hammer of his Colt. "Far enough, lady. You know something, your boyfriend, he should watch his drinking. He lets his guard down when he ties one on. Damn, but this is too easy."

Barabbas backstepped into Billy's room.

Billy growled, "You bastard!"

Jessie stepped into Billy's room just as the bounty hunter grabbed the boy by the shoulder.

"One more step, lady," Barabbas warned, "I'll blow his brains out. Dead or alive, doesn't make any difference to me. I'll still collect. Hey, whore, it's all about pride, right? Didn't I tell you? Don't fuck with me."

Jessie steeled herself, stared Barabbas dead in the eye, and told him, "I don't think you're going anywhere but straight from Hell and into the real one."

★
Chapter 17

Jessie's gaze flickered to the secret passageway to Billy's room. The door was open, revealing the bounty hunter's arrival.

Suddenly, Billy shoved himself away from Barabbas.

Jessie's revolver snaked from her holster.

Barabbas's look of confidence turned to fear and pain as Jessie shot him in the stomach.

The Colt cannoned in the bounty hunter's hand.

Wood slivers sprayed Jessie's face as the bullet tore into the doorway beside her.

Barabbas, now looking stunned, staggered back.

Jessie emptied her revolver into Barabbas, fanning the hammer, making the bounty hunter dance, twitch, and spin as a line of ragged red holes marched across his chest, spattering his face with blood.

Finally, smoke curling from the muzzle of her

revolver, her Colt held in a rock-steady grip, Jessie looked Barabbas in his fading gaze of shock.

The bounty hunter teetered, his bloody lips quivering as if he wanted to say something. The Colt slipped from his fingers and he collapsed in a heap, staring wide-eyed at the ceiling.

Grumbling a curse, Bull stumbled into the doorway behind Jessie. "Damn, but I wanted his ass for myself!" Bull growled an oath. "But good job, anyway. Outstanding! Outstanding work!"

Jessie showed Bull a grim grin, then glanced at Ki, who hadn't moved the whole time she was gunning the bounty hunter down.

Jessie opened the Colt's cylinder, dumped the empties, reloaded, spun the revolver, and tucked it neatly in her holster. "Thanks, Ki, for letting me have him. I feel a little cleaner now. Damn near like a virgin."

After Bull had dumped the body of Barabbas out in the street, he returned to his room. He said, "Jessie, Ki, I think it best if you take William and leave. Now. I stay here. Bull will deal with those four."

Jessie agreed, but Billy protested, "Bull, no! Go with us! I won't leave without you!"

"William!" Bull snapped. "No. Go."

Jessie took a step toward Billy. "Listen to him, Billy. Like the man I just killed, those four will not rest until they have either killed everyone here to get you or are themselves killed."

Jessie interrupted herself to sniff the air. She

smelled kerosene, a stench so powerful and piercing she felt nauseous.

Jessie, Ki, and Bull looked at each other, frozen for a second, then raced out into the saloon. They froze again, stared through the window, saw the fire whoosh to life down the boardwalk.

And beyond the window, outlined in firelight, stood the tall, broad shadows of the Four Horsemen.

Bull snatched up the shotgun from behind the bar. There was no time to wake the whores, but Bull hollered upstairs that the place was on fire. The saloon, Jessie knew, would burn to the ground in a matter of minutes. And she knew what the four bounty hunters had planned: Flush them out by fire, then gun them down like rats in a barrel.

Jessie grabbed Billy. "Come on!"

With Billy in tow, Jessie followed Ki and Bull into the passageway.

Moments later, they were behind the burning building, then they reached the far end of the street, rounding the corner of the buildings. There, they crouched, watching as a mountain of fire lit the night.

Revolver in hand, Jessie told Billy, "Stay here!"

"Do what she says!" Bull growled at Billy, who looked set to argue.

Jessie looked down the street.

The Four Horsemen stood there, side by side in the middle of the street, grim, tall, and silent, waiting to flush out their rats with Winchester rifles in hand.

Jessie spotted the preacher, standing behind the Four Horsemen. As he watched the flames consuming the saloon named Hell, he laughed, his eyes glowing in the firelight.

"Yes! God is just! The evil ones are punished! As they murdered, they, too, are stung by the poison of their own evil! Burn, ye evil ones, burn, burn, burn!"

Slowly, the Four Horsemen turned. The pale rider, in a laughing voice, announced, "Man of God, thus I say unto you, you shit from a horse's ass, praise be to this lord of yours."

Then the Four Horsemen cut loose with their rifles, emptying so many bullets into the preacher that the man became a bloody sieve. Rifles flamed and cracked. They poured it on the preacher, driving him, dancing, across the street, where he finally toppled in a bloody pile of twitching meat.

The pale rider spat very casually, chuckled, told the red rider, "As you implied, sir, his God could not save him from death. Thus the foolish and the self-righteous know the final power of our sword."

Jessie heard the insane, high-pitched giggle from the midget and spotted him on the hotel steps, jumping up and down, clapping his hands.

The Four Horsemen casually reloaded, as the screams of women knifed through the roaring crackle of fire.

The midget giggled and clapped.

Jason, Rufus, and Pete ran out into the street, eyes wide, staring at the fire. Just like they had killed the preacher, the Four Horsemen turned and shot the remaining happy hour crew, hammering their convulsing bodies into each other. Their screams of agony ripped apart the night for a few seconds before they fell and lay utterly still in a bloody pile in the snow.

Whores, half-dressed, and their johns began barreling out the door of Hell.

The midget howled with hysterical laughter.

One by one, as Jessie, Ki, and Bull ran to close the killing gap, the Four Horsemen shot the whores and the johns, flinging them back into the flames.

Screaming.

Gunshots.

Crackling of fire.

Giggling.

The plate-glass window to Hell shattered as two men dove out into the street, then were cut down by a volley of rifle fire.

"Nooo!" Bull shouted, running toward them, ahead of Jessie and Ki.

The Four Horsemen turned and fired at Bull. Several wild shots, fired past Bull, forced Jessie and Ki to duck for cover behind a beam a split second before wood chunks were blasted off above their faces.

Bull's shotgun erupted, nearly sawing the pale rider in half as an explosion of blood and innards washed over the snow.

The midget stopped giggling.

With a terrible relentlessness, the surviving horsemen emptied their revolvers and rifles into

Bull, sending him stumbling back, pitching across the boardwalk as the awning collapsed above him in a fiery shower.

Jessie and Ki marched ahead, as the three horsemen continued to rain death over those fleeing the burning saloon, not even glancing at their dead comrade. Two shrieking flaming banshees, slapping at their faces and bodies, ran from the fire. They were allowed to burn to death, as the horsemen kept pouring lead into whores running from Hell.

The red rider had to reload.

The three horsemen turned, spotting the shadows of Jessie and Ki.

Jessie shot the red rider once in the head, knocking him off his feet.

The midget wailed in horror.

Standing their ground side by side, Jessie and Ki unleashed a crackling din of revolver fire, ripping open the coats of the final two horsemen, shredding their chests in crimson explosions. The revolvers of the horsemen flamed and cracked impotent rounds toward the sky as they toppled backward.

Billy ran up behind Jessie and Ki, screaming, "Bull! Bull!"

Jessie pulled him away from the flames that consumed Bull's body. "Billy, no! No! He's gone, Billy!"

Billy wailed, fell to his knees, and wept.

With a groaning of wood, the saloon named Hell collapsed. Flames, soot, and debris washed across the street.

Then, from behind the saloon, there was an explosion as kerosene ignited.

Jessie stood, still as a statue, listening to Billy's sobbing, to the cleansing crackle of fire.

Jessie stared into the fires of Hell.

Then the midget, shrieking his outrage, pulled a revolver, almost as big as he was, from his holster. Ki, whirling, sent a *shuriken* flying through the air.

The midget screamed and fell as the throwing star speared into his hand.

★

Chapter 18

In grim silence, with their backs to the fires of Apocalypse, Jessie, Ki, and Billy rode east, in a slow and solemn march.

With tears in his eyes, Billy turned. Jessie followed his gaze.

It was dawn, and a dirty light had washed over the mountains, the morning lit brilliantly in the distance by the fire, which had now consumed the entire town.

Jessie had set fire to the hotel, telling herself there must be no trace of this evil place left standing.

The midget, crying, "Oh, no, what shall I do now?" over and over, had ridden out of town, into the mist to the west. "Why not just kill me, too?" he wailed over and over.

Thus the dead were left where they had died.

And all were dead. Or so Jessie believed.

Perhaps a half-hour later, they found him.

"Bull!" Billy cried, leaping off his horse.

They found him, slumped and bloody, braced against the trunk of a tree. He was scorched and black with soot. Bull groaned, lifting a bottle of whiskey to his lips.

As Jessie and Ki dismounted, Bull collapsed on his side, a stream of blood and vomit pouring from his mouth. He gagged, croaked, shuddered.

The three of them crouched beside Bull, whose naked torso was covered with blood. Blood spilled from Bull's lips. He stared at Jessie and Ki, then finally at Billy.

"Go—with them—live—"

Then Bull died, clutching his bottle of whiskey. Jessie only hoped the Great One had mercy on the soul of this strange and tormented man who had loved his whiskey and his whores and his cigarettes and the genius that is great art.

Billy wept, holding Bull in his arms.

Jessie shut her eyes, fighting back the tears.

Later in the morning, as they rode solemnly on, with Bull's body draped over the back of Jessie's mount, Ki said, "You two go on ahead."

Jessie looked at Ki, smiled, and nodded. "We can wait for you."

Ki returned Jessie's solemn smile. "That's okay. Take him with you, Jessie. I need some time alone. You'll be all right now."

"We'll wait for you in that town—you know the one."

"About a day's ride south. Yes. All right, I'll meet you there."

Jessie touched the side of Ki's face. "Remember what I said. I will never hurt you again."

With that, Jessie rode off with Billy, leaving Ki behind.

Ki rode up on Cassandra's cabin. He found her, standing by her pot, but facing him this time, as if she'd been waiting for him. She smiled, but it was not a smile of joy. It was a sad smile.

Ki stopped in front of her.

"Who are you?" he asked her. "Who are you really?"

She became grim. "I am everyone, Ki. And I am no one."

Uncertain, Ki stared at her for several moments.

She said, "Come inside. Stay with me awhile. We will know joy and happiness, if only for awhile. Then you will leave and never return here."

"Why? Why do you say that?"

"There is no why. There is only the end of all things."

Ki was sad for a moment at the thought of never seeing her again, but he sensed her power, the power that had shown him the future, and again, he was mesmerized by her beauty.

She took his hand, and Ki dismounted.

He went into her home to know joy and happiness, if only for awhile.

Watch for

**LONE STAR
IN THE SIERRA DIABLOS**

144th novel in the exciting LONE STAR series
from Jove

Coming in August!

If you enjoyed this book, subscribe now and get...

TWO FREE

A $7.00 VALUE–

If you would like to read more of the very best, most exciting, adventurous, action-packed Westerns being published today, you'll want to subscribe to True Value's Western Home Subscription Service.

Each month the editors of True Value will select the 6 very best Westerns from America's leading publishers for special readers like you. You'll be able to preview these new titles as soon as they are published, *FREE* for ten days with no obligation!

TWO FREE BOOKS

When you subscribe, we'll send you your first month's shipment of the newest and best 6 Westerns for you to preview. With your first shipment, two of these books will be yours as our introductory gift to you absolutely *FREE* (a $7.00 value), regardless of what you decide to do. If

you like them, as much as we think you will, keep all six books but pay for just 4 at the low subscriber rate of just $2.75 each. If you decide to return them, keep 2 of the titles as our gift. No obligation.

Special Subscriber Savings

When you become a True Value subscriber you'll save money several ways. First, all regular monthly selections will be billed at the low subscriber price of just $2.75 each. That's at least a savings of $4.50 each month below the publishers price. Second, there is never any shipping, handling or other hidden charges—*Free home delivery*. What's more there is no minimum number of books you must buy, you may return any selection for full credit and you can cancel your subscription at any time. A TRUE VALUE!

A special offer for people who enjoy reading the best Westerns published today.

WESTERNS!

NO OBLIGATION

Mail the coupon below

To start your subscription and receive 2 FREE WESTERNS, fill out the coupon below and mail it today. We'll send your first shipment which includes 2 FREE BOOKS as soon as we receive it.

Mail To: **True Value Home Subscription Services, Inc. P.O. Box 5235**
120 Brighton Road, Clifton, New Jersey 07015-5235

YES! I want to start reviewing the very best Westerns being published today. Send me my first shipment of 6 Westerns for me to preview FREE for 10 days. If I decide to keep them, I'll pay for just 4 of the books at the low subscriber price of $2.75 each; a total $11.00 (a $21.00 value). Then each month I'll receive the 6 newest and best Westerns to preview Free for 10 days. If I'm not satisfied I may return them within 10 days and owe nothing. Otherwise I'll be billed at the special low subscriber rate of $2.75 each; a total of $16.50 (at least a $21.00 value) and save $4.50 off the publishers price. There are never any shipping, handling or other hidden charges. I understand I am under no obligation to purchase any number of books and I can cancel my subscription at any time, no questions asked. In any case the 2 FREE books are mine to keep.

Name _____

Street Address _____ Apt. No. _____

City _____ State _____ Zip Code _____

Telephone _____

Signature _____
(if under 18 parent or guardian must sign)

Terms and prices subject to change. Orders subject to acceptance by True Value Home Subscription Services, Inc.

11048-1